AF419219

Gingerbread

Ana Ash

Copyright © 2023 Ashley Aikey

All rights reserved.

ISBN-13: 979-8-218-14762-4

To my Muse,
I first met you as a knight—handsome, fierce, and determined—then a loving husband, a warrior, and even a spy. I had no idea how much of an impact you'd have on me, and I'm so grateful. You've been the light in a terribly dark and difficult time, and writing this story got me through most of it, even when I wanted to give up. Sebastian wouldn't exist without your incredible influence, and I can't put into words just how much of an inspiration you've been, so all I can do is let my writing speak for me. (And, wow, do I really hope you don't mind being the inspiration for something kinky.) Even though you don't know who I am and may never read this, I want to thank you for being you, and I hope you find all the joy, love, and fulfillment you seek in life. Thank you for brightening my world and giving life to Sebastian and, in many ways, Gwen.

~A

Acknowledgments

Thank you, Angela, Chantelle, and Jocelyn, for putting up with my half-baked short story idea that turned into this gem of a project. Thank you for your feedback, encouragement, and unwavering confidence in me. Without the three of you, Gingerbread might never have been finished.

Thank you to everyone who helped in ways they may not even have been aware of. The little things mean more than we often given them credit for.

And another thank you to Chantelle for bringing my covers to life. One day I'll gain some digital art and photo manipulation skills. Maybe. (Ok, probably not.)

Please read before, you know, reading.

Dear reader,

I find myself in this final stage having to add a note. One of my beta readers said something that struck me as weird, and it occurred to me that those who aren't familiar with the BDSM community and lifestyle might come away with the wrong impression in some places. There are a lot of misconceptions about BDSM, and I certainly won't be able to address or dispel them all, but this is one that I need to at least try to make clear. No one, and I do mean *no one,* in this story is a sex worker of any kind. Just because someone is a dominant, it doesn't mean they're a professional Dom(me), nor that they are a sex worker. Just because someone performs at a club or an event, it doesn't mean they're a sex worker. There are plenty of situations where people share their skills in order to educate and train others, and there are plenty of situations where people put on shows for fun and even to show off what they can do. Try to think of it like going to an art gallery or a museum. So, again, no one in this story is a sex worker. Gwen is not, nor has ever been, a sex worker, and Sebastian isn't stupid enough to mistake her show in one scene for sex work. (Does he get a little jealous? Sure. The man ain't perfect.)

I'll also add that just because you know or suspect someone of being into the lifestyle, it doesn't give you the right to treat them any differently. You might know someone is into humiliation and degradation, but that doesn't give you the right to humiliate or degrade them. You might know someone is into physical pain, but that doesn't give you the right to cause them pain. You might know someone is dominant, but that doesn't give you the right to demand they boss you around or "prove it." Everything within BDSM hinges on communication, trust, and *consent.* Doing anything to anyone without their consent is ***abuse***. Should I put that in all caps or is it clear enough? Also, unless someone gives you clear, firm, enthusiastic consent while they are in full control and can make an informed decision, it's a no. If they are incapacitated in any way, they are unable to give consent, so don't be a douche-hole and take advantage of the situation. If they give a hesitant yes, it's still a no. If consent is coerced or forced, it's a no. Respect the boundaries of others.

Another note I need to add is in regards to the Australian slang and colloquialisms I've included. Finding a reliable resource online proved challenging. Some conflicted with each other, some didn't have words I'd found elsewhere, and none of them really indicated whether a word is still in use or outdated. I was informed one of my favorites is considered a bit outdated, but I love it too much to change. I'm also aware there's a great deal more swearing and certain words are used casually in Australian culture that would be considered very inappropriate by American standards. So, in order to keep the language readable and respectable for my audience, I've limited the amount of—oh, what to call it— "Aussie-speak" in the story. For those who are well-versed in it, I apologize if I've used anything incorrectly. There are a few terms provided at the end with translations, but I doubt I got them all.

So, without further ado, I give you *Gingerbread*. Think of it as my emotional support story during a rough time when I was working through some shit, and just enjoy.

~A

1

Sugar and Spice

January 12th

"Where have you brought me?" Light flakes of snow floated through the air around them and Sebastian pulled his jacket tighter against the cold. "And why are we coming in winter?" He was having second thoughts about joining his friend for a night out. They stood in front of a simple black door set into a long brick wall painted dark purple and bookended by a couple of local specialty shops. The door itself seemed random and inconspicuous except for a neon sign hanging overhead with "the Collared Heart" in purple letters. An O-ring collar wrapped around the outline of a pink heart nestled between the words.

"It's called a club, Aussie, and it's a good one. We're coming now because my heart is recently broken and getting out of the apartment will help me get back on the old horse. Lucky it's a weeknight, otherwise there'd be a line halfway down the block." Melvin shrugged and put on his most unconcerned expression. "I came here a lot before my ex entered the picture."

"Not worried we'll bump into her?"

"Nah. She's not much of a club-goer." He pushed Sebastian toward the door, deflecting the attention from his own drama. "C'mon, Bash, you promised. Think of it as a chance to unwind from work! You gotta stop burying yourself in it all the time. It's unhealthy." Melvin wagged a finger at him and tried to sound stern. "You'll be old before your time."

"Uh huh. And what kind of club is this again?"

"The fun kind. Hey, Mike." Melvin nodded to the hulking bouncer who waved them through. "You're going to like it."

"Yeah, right." Sebastian seriously doubted that. He avoided clubs and bars on principle—too many people, too much noise. *But I promised. Damn it.*

The cold dissipated once they were inside. He found himself in a well-ordered lobby that reminded him of a hotel more than the usual club entrance he expected. A large, black board occupied one eggplant-colored wall with an array of paper announcements neatly spread out over it. Some mentioned events coming to the club, others gave dates and times for classes, and there was a two-month calendar done in bright chalks. Sebastian squinted to read more details, but Melvin ushered him along. A petite woman with mousy-brown hair and cat-eyed spectacles stood patiently behind a warm walnut counter. Sebastian waved his hand, gesturing to the room in general. "Not exactly what I thought I'd see for the inside of a club. What is this, Mel?"

"Where we sign in, obviously."

"Hello, Melvin, it's been a while since you last came, but I doubt you've forgotten how this works." The woman tapped an open sign-in book with bright pink nails that matched the pinstripes on her black suit. "Member card and signature, please."

"Naturally, Miss Renee." Melvin dug his wallet out and presented a matte-black card with the club's logo in purple and pink on one side. "My friend here is dipping his toes into the pond tonight, so if you have the papers handy…."

"Of course." Renee pulled a folder from a drawer somewhere below the counter and set it in front of Sebastian with a pen. "These are standard consent and liability forms, which must be filled out completely before you can go back. They're only good for tonight as a guest pass, and if you should decide you want to become a member, there's a different set of forms."

"Uh. Consent and liability?" Sebastian flipped through the papers, trying to understand what his friend was getting him into before going back and reading them carefully. *BDSM? Dungeon? "You are responsible for your own safety. Remember the rules of communication and consent and have fun." What kind of "club" has Mel brought me to? He's dead set on getting me outside my comfort zone tonight.* He sighed and signed in the appropriate places and presented his license while Renee made sure everything was in order.

"I'll take your coats as well. Remember to pick them up when you leave and enjoy your night at the Collared Heart." She smiled and waved them toward another black door.

"Thank you, Miss!" Melvin grabbed Sebastian's arm and tugged him through. "C'mon, man, this is going to be fun!"

"I'm still not sure what you've gotten me into, but since we're already here." The first thing he noticed once they stepped into the main room was the lack of bass vibrating his skull. The music was loud, but its rhythm was distinguishable, and he could easily pick out the lyrics if he half-paid attention. The second thing was a skinny young man in a short, purple-and-pink vinyl maid outfit, black stockings, and pink chunky heels coming toward them, loaded tray in hand.

"Mel!" The maid quickened his pace until he could jab a finger in Melvin's chest. "Where have you been? I've been. *So. Worried.* About you, Muffin."

"I'm sorry, I've just been so busy." Melvin's voice rose a couple octaves, and he batted his lashes at the maid.

"*Mhm.* I'm sure you have. And where is *le girlfriend?*" His nose scrunched as if smelling something foul.

"Ah, well, you know...."

"Aw. I know I should say I'm sorry and sympathize, but she wasn't good for you. You can do much better. Oh-em-gee." His face lit up. "Then tonight's a great night to be here. There are a *lot* of single Dommes, and I'm *sure* you'll meet someone."

"Mm sounds awfully tempting and exactly what I need, but we'll see. This is my friend, Sebastian. We're out on the town tonight."

"Hi, handsome. Is this your first time to the Collared Heart?"

"Uh, nah yeah, it is. Mel wanted some company."

"Ooo that accent. Mm." He bit his lip and gave Sebastian a slow once over. "Attached?"

"Come on, give the man some room to breathe before you try to seduce him."

The maid gasped and swatted at Melvin. "You make me sound like some kind of man-eater."

"If the stiletto fits…. Kidding! I'm kidding. Don't pout. Would you be a sweetheart and bring us a scotch and a bourbon? Please?" Melvin shooed him away and took Sebastian by the elbow. "Let's go to one of the tables by the border."

"The border?"

"It's a half-wall separating the area up here from the lower floor. There's usually at least one free table there, and it'll give you a nice view of the main stage. There's no show tonight, but you can see more of the people here and get a better sense of the club."

"Mel, I, uh…. This place is…different. Can you just catch me up, please?" They stopped at a bar-height table. "Maybe give me a chair? Oxygen?"

"Bash, relax." Melvin took their drinks from the maid and passed Sebastian the bourbon. "Why don't you take a few to soak it all up? Give your mind a chance to process while you enjoy your drink, and then I'll answer some of those questions burning a hole in your brain."

"Fine." Sebastian sipped his drink and tried to take in everything. On the inside, the Collared Heart was more than just a niche night club, it was a full dinner theater with booths and tables across the lower floor. A black curtain hung across the stage, dimly illuminated by purple and pink lights, and a large crowd of people spread out over the shiny dance floor in front of it. *Seems busy for a Thursday night, must be pretty popular. Is that a…nah.* He cleared his throat uncertainly. "So, Mel, you know we could have gone to a regular bar, gotten drinks, and bemoaned the state of our love lives. Why did you bring me here, to a…uh…a fetish club, or whatever you call it?"

"We don't need to wallow. We need to find new girlfriends. Or you do. It's been long enough since the last one."

"I thought we came here for you."

"Sure, but there's no reason you can't enjoy yourself, too, and if you happen to meet a nice woman or find a new hobby, all the better." Melvin watched a few women walk by. "Just give it a try. You might like it."

"Like what exactly? Drinking and people watching?" He rolled his eyes.

"*No*. You're always in control, Bash, and you never really...." Melvin waved his hands around, searching for the right wording. "You're always 'on.' When was the last time you had a decent night's sleep? Or *actually* relaxed? Honestly?"

"I don't know. I have a lot to do."

"Because you refuse to delegate anything. You don't need to be in control all the time and falling asleep at your desk isn't a healthy habit. Take a moment to unwind and let someone else be in charge for a while."

"You mean let a stranger tie me up and boss me around?"

"I mean, that's...putting it absurdly simple. There's so much more to it. Watch." A woman in shiny red vinyl and spiked heels walked up, and Melvin smiled dreamily at her. "Hi."

"Hello, there. You're very cute." She was a cat about to pounce on a tasty morsel. "Belong to anyone?"

"Afraid I'm recently available and in need of consoling." Melvin puffed out his lower lip and blinked pitifully.

"You poor thing. I can help you with you that if you want." She smoothed his auburn hair back. "What about your friend?"

"Oh, nah, I'm good. But thank you." Sebastian couldn't figure out what else to say and decided it was better to keep his mouth shut.

"Well, try to have some fun then." Melvin stood and linked arms with his new friend.

"Wait! Where are you going?"

"To be consoled, obviously. You sure you don't want to come?"

"I came here for you, because you said you didn't want to go out alone and needed a friend. I didn't come to meet new people or hookup. Or sit here by myself."

"Relax a little, Bash. Be open."

"I'll tell you what," the woman interjected, "we'll check in on you in a little bit, and if you're still here and still lonely, we'll figure something else out."

"Fine. Go...have your fun, Mel."

"Thanks, man." Melvin smiled and let her lead him to another table.

I can't believe him. All that "oh, poor me, please hang out with me," and he just goes off with some random person. Sebastian snatched his drink from the table and glanced over the crowd "I hate clubs," he muttered. *I'll just finish my drink and go.* A woman in leather walked by leading a man dressed as a horse by a leash. *I do not belong here. I—* The crowd of people on the floor below shifted, and a woman in a deep blue corset and short, black skirt appeared. Her lips caught his attention. They were a shiny, peacock sort of blue, and she kept her dark hair swept back in a loose, elegant bun. His eyes followed the curve of her neck, down her bust, waist, and hips to the smooth leather boots that disappeared under the bottom of her skirt. "Damn." Sebastian's breath caught his throat. *I hope she's the good kind of trouble. Shit, is she looking at me?*

The woman smirked and wove through the people to the stairs, hips swaying hypnotically with each step she took toward him. Although many watched her pass by, no one stopped her, and each maid curtsied and moved out of the way. Her presence commanded respect and obedience. When she reached Sebastian's table, she leaned back against the railing, using her forearms to support most of her weight, and tilted her head to better see his face. "Hi. I don't believe I've seen you here before."

"Oh, i-it's my first time. Here." *Why am I stuttering? I haven't tripped over my own tongue in front of a woman since…since forever.*

"Hm. You're Australian?" Her voice was soft moonlight and a tempting invitation to give in.

"I am. Is that a problem?"

"Not at all. In fact, I'm very fond of non-American accents." She grinned and bit her lip. "I'm Gwen."

"Sebastian."

"What part of Australia are you from?"

"I grew up in Newcastle, right on the eastern coast. Lots of surfing and Sydney's only two hours away."

"You enjoy surfing?"

"Absolutely. Not much of that here though. What about you?"

"I'm from Upstate, near Saratoga, but I've lived in the city for a while now."

"It's exciting here. Always something to do and tons of opportunities. Take this place. I'd never heard of it before tonight." Sebastian caught himself staring at her lips again. *Stop that. She's going to think you're a creeper. Make eye contact, pay attention, don't drool. Her lips are just so….* "You have beautiful li—I mean eyes. You have beautiful eyes." He groaned. "I'm sorry. I don't know what's wrong with me. I swear I'm not normally this awkward."

"Don't worry, I'm not going to hold it against you." Gwen gave him a disarming smile.

"So, I am very new to all of this. Are you a—what's the word?"

"Why don't I just lay it out so we're clear from the start?"

"That would be appreciated. Like, *truly* appreciated, because I'm so lost right now."

"I'll bet you are, handsome." Gwen licked her blue-coated lips. "You look good enough to eat, especially with that easily-spooked vibe. Like a puppy."

"You eat puppies?"

"Only when they're good boys." Her smile broadened as his cheeks flushed. "Adorable."

"Thanks, I think. It's just my friend left me, and I'm…never mind. I'm just making it worse." He pushed a hand through his dark blond hair.

"Mhm." She watched him shift uncomfortably. "I'm a Domme, female, straight, monogamous, and unattached. You?"

"Straight, male, monogamous, and unattached. I don't know about the other thing."

"Well, you don't strike me as particularly dominant."

"Really? But I own and operate a large company. Wouldn't that make me more likely to be dominant?"

"That doesn't make you dominant, sweetness. Plenty of high-end, hard-working CEOs are submissive behind closed doors. Allowing someone else to be in control for a while gives them a chance to relax."

"I guess that makes sense. Then what *would* make me dominant?"

"There's something about the way you carry yourself. You don't have the attitude."

"Maybe I'm just nervous." Sebastian finished his drink.

"Oh, you're definitely nervous—you look ready to run. But, in my experience, most guys who are new to the scene and fancy themselves dominants tend to posture a lot, *especially* when they're nervous. It gives them the illusion of control." Gwen took the empty glass from his hands and got a maid's attention. "He'll have another," she sniffed the contents, "bourbon on the rocks."

"Thanks. Shouldn't I be getting your drink though?"

"I'm good. I don't drink much when I go out."

"That's fair. So, you're a Domme and I'm a...what?"

"Remains to be discovered. Why don't you tell me about your last relationship?"

"Um, ok." He shrugged, not sure how relevant it was. "My ex was a bit of a priss, demanding, and always made me take the lead. I had to do everything. It was exhausting after working all day. Constantly on the go, out as often as possible to eat or shop or go to a party. And the *texting*. I don't mind some. I'm all for talking and knowing what's going on, but not every minuscule detail, and not when I've already said I'm in an important meeting and *can't* talk. She called my office once when I didn't reply right away and accused me of cheating, but I was in a meeting with some investors—which I'd told her I would be. It was a nightmare, and we almost lost the deal. She always wanted more, and nothing I gave was ever enough."

"What made you stop?"

"My brother. He had enough of it and decided to knock some sense into me. Literally. We got into a fist fight over her, and we're not violent people." Sebastian frowned at the memory of punching and being punched by his brother. Their mother had been furious at the pair of them rolling around her fancy living room. *Didn't we break a glass vase? Or was it just the table?* "Honestly, she was never much into physical contact, in public or private. We rarely held hands or kissed, and real intimacy was...well, it was almost non-existent."

"I'm sorry. I know what it's like to be starved for affection and taken advantage of."

"I haven't dated since. Sorry, that was more information than you needed, and it probably sounds as if I'm just complaining."

"Not at all. Everyone has a dating horror story, and this gives me a clearer picture of you. What about work? What do you do that keeps you so busy?"

"Does it matter?"

"I prefer to know the competition." Gwen tilted her head to better read his expressions.

"Competition?"

"The more time you spend working, the less time and energy you have for other things. And it's not healthy to spend all your life working—that's a bad habit I'd have to deal with if you're a workaholic."

"I've been hearing that a lot today." He took a deep breath and considered what he was comfortable sharing. "I'm a businessman."

She laughed at him. "You and half the people here."

"Ah…. Fair enough. My brother and I own a company that has dealings internationally, so we have an office here in New York, one in L.A., there's one in Seattle, a couple back home, and we're breaking into the European market. And, no, I don't spend all my time working, but there are busier times than others. After the breakup, I buried myself in it a bit more than usual. What about you?"

"I'm an editor, mostly developmental stuff, and I help a couple of friends with their online publication. They do several issues a year and sometimes they need an extra pair of eyes to go through the submissions."

"You mean a magazine or books?"

"Books. The publication is short stories and poetry, but my focus for both is speculative fiction."

"Do you enjoy it?"

"I do. I love books."

"Me, too! I love a good thriller, but I'll read just about anything. What's your favorite genre?"

"Fantasy and horror, but I'm especially into anything involving mythology and folklore, too."

"What else do you like?" Sebastian barely noticed when the maid dropped off his drink. "Movies? Music? Do you have a favorite type of food?"

"So many questions. Um…well…have you had one of those moments where someone asks you about yourself, and you immediately forget everything?"

"All. The. Time. Ok, ok. How about Thai food?"

"I'm not sure I've eaten much before."

"Well, maybe you could Thai it out with me some time." He ignored the maid who almost dropped their tray in a fit of giggles and focused on keeping a straight face. "I know a great little restaurant."

Gwen closed her eyes and turned her head away for a minute, pursing her lips and trying not to laugh. "Hm. The man makes puns." *All right. I'll consider that a yellow-green flag.* "Perhaps I'll take you up on that some Thai-me. But I'm partial to ramen, fresh seafood, and a good steak."

"Sushi?"

"Of course."

"I love old, campy horror movies and swing music. Oh! Probably cliché, but also Sinatra."

"Haha. I'll take spooky movies, paranormal documentaries, and I like a pretty wide variety of music, but Sinatra and Frankie Valli are definitely on the list."

"Oh man. Yes. Yes." He clasped his hands to stop from tapping the table excitedly.

"But I have a question for you."

"I'm happy to answer anything."

"May I touch you?"

Sebastian stilled, cheeks flushing. "Uh...yeah?"

"That's not a firm yes. It's all right if you're not comfortable with it."

"I'm just...surprised you asked first." He flexed his fingers and drummed them against his thighs. "People don't usually ask if they can touch me. And I know some touching is just meant to be a friendly gesture, but that doesn't...it doesn't mean...."

"It doesn't mean it's ok." Gwen's first instinct was to reach out and comfort him, especially when he was clearly upset, but she stayed where she was. "I understand. I'm the same way, and I want you to know I'll only touch you if you're ok with it, and only where and for as long as you're ok with it."

Sebastian considered. This stranger was asking his permission to touch him, and nothing about her tone made it sound as if there were a wrong answer. He thought about the business parties he and his brother frequented. All the people who would startle him from behind with an unexpected pat on the back or arm around his shoulders. The ones who would grab his arm or hand and haul him through the room to meet more people who wanted to touch him.

"It's a weird predicament, isn't it? Wanting physical affection but not wanting to be touched."

"Yeah. Socially, we're obligated to tolerate it in some situations."

"Usually by the time we realize it's ok to set boundaries, we have those people who're used to being in our space, assumed it was and still is fine, and get mad when we try to enforce our limits." Gwen shrugged. "It's fine until we take back something they felt entitled to."

He pursed his lips, fingers still going. "Where did you want to touch me?"

"Your chin."

"All right."

"My shoulder might touch yours, since we're already standing so close."

"Ok." Sebastian stood still and watched the light play across Gwen's features as she sidled closer and angled her body until their shoulders were touching. The heat in his cheeks deepened as she traced the small scar cutting through the short, coarse hairs on the right side of his chin before her fingers gently cupped his face.

"How's this?"

"I'm not sure I understand." He swallowed hard and took a steadying breath. "Is that...jasmine?"

"Mhm. Wisteria and jasmine. How do I make you feel? In this moment?"

"Uh-m." Sebastian tried to order his thoughts. *I love jasmine. Reminds me of home, but the wisteria.... How can someone smell comforting and sexy at the same time?* He wanted to run his hands along her curves and kiss her. "I'm nervous and not sure what to make of what's going on in my head."

"Are you uncomfortable?"

"Nah, not at all. I'm...." He thought about the mix of emotions and sensations rushing through him. Gwen's gaze was patient, her hand steady as her fingers caressed his jaw on the way to run through his hair. "You're so calm. It makes me at ease and terribly curious. I think I'm only anxious because this is new, and we're in public."

"Do you want me to stop?"

"No."

"Then it's a good thing."

"Yeah, definitely. I'm also...eager? I'm not sure that's the right word. I don't know if that makes any sense." Absently, he nuzzled her hand when it slid up his cheek.

"It does." She pulled her hand away and tucked a stray lock of long dark hair behind her ear. "You said eager. What do you mean by that? Or are you not sure?"

"Eager to...I don't know. I guess I want to know more and

possibly figure out if this could be something I'd enjoy."

"In general? Or is there something in particular you want to know if you'd enjoy?"

He shrugged casually and mumbled, "being yours."

"I'm sorry, I didn't quite catch that." She grinned mischievously.

"Being yours. If I'd enjoy being yours." Sebastian's face burned and he tried to cover his embarrassment with a drink.

"That's one of the cutest things anyone has ever said to me."

"I'm not used to feeling this way."

"Hm. All right. Come." She held her hand out.

He trailed after her, delighted by the warmth of his hand in hers as she deftly wove through the crowd to the lower area. They passed Melvin who sent Sebastian a smug grin and continued chatting enthusiastically with the Domme in red. *He's going to have fun with this. I can hear it now. But she's definitely worth any grief Mel gives me later.* "Where are we going?"

"Somewhere we can speak a little more privately." The Collared Heart was dotted with nooks and crannies built in for those seeking privacy in the middle of a popular night club. Gwen located an empty alcove and settled into a deep, eggplant-purple booth and motioned for Sebastian to take the seat opposite her. The half-enclosed space was angled so they could easily watch the stage, although it was slated to remain empty for the night, and she tugged a sheer curtain covered in little hearts across the opening to indicate they were having a closed meeting. "I find you intriguing, Sebastian, and you seem interested in learning more. So, I was hoping you might be open to talking."

"Talking?"

"Just talking for now. Trust, communication, and consent are basic tenants in BDSM, and you can't give informed consent without first communicating and establishing a basis of trust."

"And what if I decide I'm not into all this?" He waved his hand toward the scene beyond the curtain.

"That's fine, at least there's the possibility of a nice conversation. But are you saying you're not into this?" She gestured to herself and raised her eyebrows.

"Well, you're a different matter entirely. You're gorgeous. And those *boots*." Sebastian's eyes wandered from her toes, up her crossed legs, pausing at the edge of her skirt before darting back up to her face. "I love what you're wearing, and it's hard not to stare."

"I'm glad. You're practically drooling." Gwen pressed her back into the cushion and watched him self-consciously wipe at his mouth.

"No. I'm just appreciating."

"It's nice to be appreciated. You probably have questions."

"I have *many*."

"Pick one and we'll go from there."

"Ok." He wanted to tease her a bit, and the question rolled off his tongue before he could decide against it. "You're a Domme, so, if I misbehave, are you going to spank me?"

"Do you like being spanked?"

"Uh." His cheeky grin disappeared. "No, actually, I don't. I'm not particularly fond of pain in general." Sebastian realized he forgot his drink at the other table and played with the idea of ordering another just to have something to do with his hands. "I honestly don't know anything about all of this," he said, gesturing to the room again, "except what I've seen in movies or weird porn. I'm sorry if I offended you with my question."

"You didn't. It's a pretty common expectation."

"Don't you already have a, uh, a...what's it called again?" Disarmed by her smile, Sebastian leaned closer and propped his elbows on the small table.

"A submissive?" She shook her head. "I have a particular style that doesn't work for a lot of people in this world, and even those who are on board with it still generally want things I'm not interested in doing."

"I don't understand."

"I'm straight, monogamous, and not a sadist. I don't like pegging, and while I do like dictating what my sub wears from time to time, I don't do forced feminization or objectification. Don't get me wrong, I'll punish you for misbehaving, but we'd work out what's acceptable first."

"You don't just decide everything?"

"No, but that's one of media's favorite parts of the stereotype. A vinyl-clad Dominant, crop in hand, standing over a bound and gagged submissive who looks appropriately terrified."

"Oh, so you mean it's not like—" Sebastian stopped talking when

Gwen put a finger over his lips.

"Not even close." She sat back again. "Don't trust anything Hollywood feeds you on the subject. It's ironic that anything providing an inaccurate representation of a group, no matter how big, small, well-known, or obscure they are, is popularized and accepted as the 'expert' source. I've tried to read a lot of books that marketed themselves as kinky, tried watching movies, but they're always so awful I can't bring myself to finish them. Eventually, I stopped, and I've heard more than enough about all the problems with certain popular fiction from colleagues who aren't even a part of the kink community."

"Problems?"

"Where do I start? Problem number one is most writers don't take the time to show the non-sexy parts of BDSM."

"There are non-sexy parts?"

"Mhm, and one of them is what we're doing right now. Talking, getting to know one another, establishing boundaries and limitations. They also tend to skip over negotiations and aftercare, both of which are very important parts. But I could forgive that if the relationships being depicted weren't inherently abusive more often than not."

"I see. Well, not that I've watched or read much of them myself, but I would think it'd be bad to promote abusive relationships as healthy."

"Media doesn't care. Whatever makes them the most money. As for people who are watching and reading these stories not being disturbed by it, the man is often rich and good-looking, which means he can do no wrong. It's fine for him to stalk and try to control the person he's after. When something from his past is revealed as being the reason for why he's the way he is and even why he's into the life, it somehow excuses everything and, honestly, makes the community look bad. 'Oh, poor him, he's just broken and needs a good woman to love and fix him.' But you *can't* fix someone, you can't make them change, so the happy ending is a sham. And even in fiction a sham is a sham, but since it fits with what we've been trained to believe is acceptable and desirable in a partner, questioning it means getting weird looks and being ostracized. The man is handsome, rich, and powerful, and he uses his damage as an excuse for how he treats his partner. Now, if he weren't handsome or rich, he'd be labeled as a creepy stalker and a narcissistic, psychologically abusive individual."

"The unattractive guy showing interest is off-putting, while advances from the handsome one are welcome, no matter his personality or reputation." Sebastian peered through the gauzy curtain and watched the fuzzy shapes of people moving by. "And it's not abuse, because 'hey, it's kinky and she's into that, so obviously she wanted it.' Psychological abuse still isn't considered 'real' abuse by most people."

"Exactly. And media has romanticized this type of relationship and made it seem acceptable—desirable even. They've encouraged people to accept stalking, controlling behaviors, and psychological and emotional abuse, normalized these things, which creates a larger pool of potential victims for those kinds of people." Gwen made an apologetic face. "Sorry, I didn't mean to rant. A friend of mine was in a relationship with one of them. They had *a* nice date, and he took that as permission to show up whenever he wanted without warning or invitation. Her other friends told her she should've been flattered by the attention. I was the only one who told her to run. Three years, two kids, and one horrifying night in the ER later, it all came out."

"I see." *No wonder she takes it so seriously.* "And what about here? When you're actively surrounded by the community?"

"We still have to be careful. There are a lot of pseudo-Dominants and submissives out there, and there are a lot of people out there who think certain types of relationships are not only normal but the way it's supposed to be. As someone who is new, you need to be wary. Gender is inconsequential. I've seen FemDommes as bad as hyper-masculine Alpha Doms, and they will eat you alive if you give them an inch."

"You're not like that."

"No, but trust isn't a given. I have no right to your trust, just as you have no right to mine."

"So, what about the hitting and humiliating? Or the times when the submissive has no will of their own?"

"Everything is consensual, and a proper Domme will talk with you first, even one for hire or when it's just a single session. Negotiations are for establishing ground rules, boundaries—"

"A safe word?"

"Mhm."

"What about when someone can't speak? I've seen a lot of people in here with masks on and I'm sure the whole point of a gag is so the person *can't* talk."

"Gestures, body language, whatever they've decided on beforehand." Gwen wondered how she could put everything in terms he'd understand. *I haven't had this conversation in forever.* "Submissives have more power than most people on the outside realize."

"How so?"

"You remember the pony that walked by you earlier? I know that couple. When he needs something, he stamps his foot. Twice for when he needs to speak, like asking for a drink or to go to the bathroom, and three times if he needs to tap out. They can stop everything with a word or a gesture. The Domme can, too, but the whole idea that a submissive is utterly powerless is an illusion. It's all a power exchange —one person giving control to another. The line between power-*ful* and power-*less* can be clear or blurry, but it's good to remember consent can be easily revoked by *all* parties involved."

"Really? That seems...." Sebastian mulled it over for a moment. "So, what if the person in control doesn't want to give up the power they've been given after the submissive has said or done whatever to indicate they want to stop?"

"All of this is done with consent and once that's been retracted, you're go against someone's wishes, doing something to them they don't want, and it becomes abuse."

"What if someone forgets their safe word or gesture? When you're first starting out, can't it be hard to remember in the moment? What then?"

"That's why you don't rush. Or at least why I don't rush. And even when you've been playing together for a while you should still have check-ins with each other to make sure there aren't any problems. It's important when using things like rope because you have to keep an eye on circulation and make sure nothing is being pinched. When you're starting or trying something new, you need to check in with your partner frequently. I know it's not the sexiest part of any encounter, even if it's just sex, and people don't always want to because it might 'break the scene,' but better that than violating your partner's trust or finding yourselves in the hospital."

Sebastian was still full of questions, but one was starting to nag at him more than the others. "You seem knowledgeable and capable, and you've been generous with your time, even knowing this might not lead anywhere. So, how is it you haven't found anyone you're compatible with?"

"It's been a…difficult search, and I'm not accustomed to trusting lightly. Some people want to rush in and do everything all at once, and that's not how I operate. There's also the matter of having something in common outside of kink. I'm not a 'wham-bam-thank-you-ma'am' type. I enjoy conversation and building a real connection with my submissive."

"I see." He rubbed his jaw and tapped his foot. "And if I just wanted sex?"

"Then you're talking with the wrong woman." Gwen told herself not to be disappointed. "I don't do sex with strangers, or even casual sex with friends."

"So, sex and kink aren't interdependent?"

"They go hand-in-hand for a lot of people, but not everyone. Not for me. Will I have sex with a dedicated partner I trust? Sure, but I don't need sex to have a fulfilling scene. And I am not a…a…." She sucked in a breath.

"I'm sorry. I wasn't trying to offend you. I just…I'm sorry." Sebastian didn't know if he could save the conversation. *Damn it. Why would you ask that, you moron?* Before the silence became awkward, he rephrased his question. "What I was really trying to ask was what if I wanted to pursue something with you without all the trappings of kink involved and wanted just…regular sex?"

"Are you asking if I'd be interested in a vanilla relationship?"

"I guess. I'm not saying I'm not interested in this at all—because I am curious—but what if I find out I'm not into it? What if I wanted you? Regardless of kinky things being involved?" He put his hand on hers hesitantly. "What if I wanted to spend more time with you? Could I…take you for coffee or something?"

"Are you asking me on a date?"

"I'm asking you to tell me more about this world some place it's not so loud. I don't like clubs. Too much noise and activity. And, maybe, yes, it would be a little bit of a date," he said, stumbling over the last word.

"You're so flustered." Gwen brushed her fingers along his scruffy cheek. *He's very cute, but I don't know. What if it's just an act?* "So, to be clear, you want to take me out and get to know me better, learn more about what I'm into, and find out if there's any chance of continuing even if you don't like what I do?"

"Yes. I haven't asked a woman out in a while, so I'm not very good at it." Sebastian wanted to hide his embarrassment but kept his eyes on hers. After a minute, her expression warmed with a lopsided smile.

"Maybe there's hope for you." *Maybe it's worth the risk?* "There's something else I want to ask first. I noticed a few Dommes checking you out while you were watching me, even a few subs who probably thought you might be their type. Why not one of them?"

He didn't need to look. *It's probably the same couple of groups from earlier when Mel and I walked in.* "Well, none of them approached me, but also because I'm not interested in them, but I am in you. Only in you. What do I need to do to make it," he made a vague motion with his hands, "more obvious I want to spend time with you? Even if it's just as a friend, I'd love to talk with you, and I wouldn't mind finding out if I'm able to do this, to be this. I'd like to try."

"Hm." An idea came to Gwen, and she leaned forward conspiratorially. "Would you be up for a trial run of sorts to see if you're interested in kink? And we can decide how to proceed from there?"

"I would, yes."

"There's something we could try now, if you want."

"But what about everyone else?" He glanced nervously at the sheer curtain.

"I promise what we're going to try is *much* tamer than what usually goes on here, but I know all the places privacy can be found at the Collared Heart." She held up a silver skeleton key and bit her lip at the curiosity in Sebastian's face. *Now* that *is an adorable man.*

"Where does it lead?"

"You'll see if you follow me. Will you?"

"Yes. I can't believe I'm doing this, but yes." Sebastian pulled back the curtain and got up, squaring his shoulders. "Lead on, my lady. I'm all yours."

Gwen twined her fingers with his and led him to a door in the side wall that read "Employees Only." The stocky bouncer guarding the door smiled and leaned down so she could whisper something in his ear. He nodded and held the door open while she guided Sebastian into a narrow hallway littered with theater-related items at various intervals.

"Where are we?" Compared to the main part of the club, the colors were plain and the lighting straightforward. *The walls must have some damn good insulation. I can barely hear the music.*

"Think of this as backstage. The owner has an office here and a few rooms for private meetings or if friends need a place to stay. I thought this would be a safe place for us."

"Safe? I mean, yeah, it's quieter and not crowded, but we could have gone back to my place or yours."

"No, this is neutral ground. Neither of us has the upper hand aside from my experience, and that can make things less stressful. When you have someone unfamiliar in your private space, it can be hard to relax."

"That makes sense. Do you...come back here often?"

"All the time." Gwen glanced back and tilted her head when she felt him stop. "Wha— *Oh.* Not for this. I'm good friends with the owner, so I'm back here a lot, and sometimes I help set up for shows."

"And does the owner know we're going back here?"

"Of course. I know everything that goes on in my club," said a calm, feminine voice. A slender young man with neon green hair appeared from around the corner. "I'm Fabian, owner and manager of the Collared Heart."

"I'm Sebastian. It's nice to meet you." He shook Fabian's hand.

"Mhm, likewise. You've picked a cute one Gwen. I have to admit I'm surprised. It's been so long. Do you think the lifestyle's for him though? He seems a little...flighty."

"We're about to find out or at least get a better idea, but I think he has potential."

"Mm. Follow me then." Fabian grinned and led them further into the back of the club to a cozy lounge area and stopped in front of a plain, purple door. "Ok." He clapped excitedly. "First time in forever you've shown interest in a sub, and I'm happy to be here for this momentous occasion. Key, Dove." He unlocked the door.

"We were in one of the curtained booths, but the noise and crowd were distracting and making him anxious. Being alone would be better for this anyway." She squeezed Sebastian's hand encouragingly.

"No worries, I get it. I was nervous my first time, too. And if there'd been an audience? *Ugh*. I'd have died. Let's give the two of you some comfortable privacy. Sebastian?"

"Yes?"

"Gwen is going to ask you some questions and I need you to answer her honestly."

"All right, I can do that."

"Do you consent to be here with me?" Her voice trembled a little, but she stayed calm.

Sebastian looked down at his hand in Gwen's. "I do."

"Are you here of your own free will?"

"I am."

"Do you consent to me being your Domme for this short time? And do you consent to Fabian being nearby in order to keep an eye on things?"

"I do."

"Any health issues I should be aware of? Anything in particular you don't like or aren't comfortable with?"

"No and no, other than the spanking, which we covered earlier."

"Excellent! I'll be right here if you need me." Fabian waved the pair inside.

"Thanks, Fab. I really appreciate this."

"Yeah, thank you." Sebastian followed Gwen, curious about what she had in mind. The room was painted in pinks and purples to match the club's theme, but the darker wine tones of the bedding and the soft glow from a sconce on each wall made it more intimate. A bench upholstered in black leather stood at the foot of the queen bed. "So, what happens now?"

"Since you're new to this, we'll use the color system. If you need to slow down, say yellow, if you're ok to keep going, say green, and if, for any reason, you need to stop, say red. I'll stop immediately." Gwen let go of his hand to close the door, making sure it was open just a crack for Fabian. She sat on the bench and watched Sebastian nervously stuff his hands in his pockets.

"What are we doing?" His stomach knotted up.

"Think of this as a way to help you determine if you have any interest in me as a Domme."

"What if I don't, but find myself still enraptured by you?" *That sounded dumb. You're such an idiot, Bash, she's not going to take you seriously.*

"Enraptured? Sweet Sebastian, are you a poet?"

"Rarely, but when the muse strikes, I let her guide me where she wills." *Maybe I'm not doing so bad. This might go pretty well.* "And you're so alluring, I find myself tripping over my tongue and being poetic at the same time. I can't seem to help it."

"Well, I love poetry. You know, if you decide you don't want anything kinky but still want to take me out, I'm sure we can come to some arrangement. But we can discuss that later. For this short moment between us, allow me to be your muse." She beckoned him with a single finger.

"My muse?" He chuckled and decided to go with it. Sebastian gravitated toward her, unable and unwilling to resist Gwen's pull. "Right now, my muse appears before me as a goddess waiting to be worshipped and adored. Is that what I need to do to be inspired?" He took his blazer off and set it on the side table near the door. Slowly, he went down on one knee, then the other, and he gazed up into the warm, cognac eyes of his muse-goddess. A sense of belonging washed over him, and he found his hands reaching for her. He laid his head in her lap.

"May I touch you?"

"Mhm." As Gwen calmly stroked his hair, Sebastian's muscles relaxed, and his heart stopped racing. He was at peace for the first time in months. *I could go to sleep. Would she be mad if I did?*

"Good boy," she said, her voice quiet and encouraging. "Talk to me. Tell me how you feel right now."

He didn't answer right away. Words were slow to form, especially when he met her eyes again. "I...I...don't know. Content? I want to go to sleep."

"What do you need from me?"

"For you to...to...be my muse."

"Sebastian?" *I should've asked earlier. Shit.* "How much did you have to drink tonight? I know you barely touched the drink I ordered for you, but how much did you have before that?"

"A drink. And I had dinner an hour or two before we came." He rubbed his cheek on her lap and wrapped his arms around her legs. "Just let me stay for a while, please" he added with a sigh.

"All right."

The sensation of her hand in his hair was confident and reassuring, but it was a gentle strength that didn't push him in any direction. He languished in the faint memories stirred up by her attention. *I've missed this. Why haven't I been with anyone who likes to be this close? I used to love being affectionate with my partner.* "Does it bother you?"

"Does what bother me?"

"That I'm getting all of the attention right now."

She let out a soft, breathy laugh. "I don't think you realize how much attention you're giving me."

"What do you mean?"

"I have an attractive man who's at least six inches taller than me kneeling at my feet with his head in my lap. And, unless I'm grossly misreading the situation, he's enjoying it. That's Domme goals for me."

"Oh. I didn't think of it like that." He grew quiet again. *This can't be all there is to it. It can't be so simple.* "Is there anything I can do for you?"

"You're doing plenty."

"But how can it be enough? Tell me what I can do to make you happy."

His voice was muffled against her leg, but she could make out the pleading tone. "Right now, this is enough for me. I'm happy."

"Then how can I be yours? I want to give you more. I *need* to give you more."

"We can talk about that later, when we're both clear-headed."

"But—"

"I'll not negotiate anything more than this with you for tonight. That would be unethical and irresponsible on my part." *Big man, big sigh.* She shook her head and continued running her fingers through his hair. "Sebastian? Talk to me."

"Would it be ok if I fell asleep? I am so...damn...tired." Sebastian went slack and let out a small snore.

"Oh boy. Fab?"

"Yes, babe?" Fabian poked his head into the room. "Everything ok?"

"I broke him."

"I'm sorry. You what?"

"Kidding. Sort of. Any ideas to bring him out slowly?"

"Out? Gwen, you have enough experience to deal with—oh. Oh

wow. What did you do to the poor thing?"

"I just had him kneel at my feet. He put his head in my lap while I stroked his hair, we talked a little bit, and then...this. I don't know what his triggers are yet, but he did mention his ex-girlfriend wasn't very affectionate. And now he's just passed out."

"He is just an absolute puddle of subby-ness right now. Let's get him up." Fabian hooked one arm under Sebastian while Gwen got his other side, and together they settled him in the bed and wrapped in a weighted blanket. "He's mumbling about," Fabian leaned down to listen. "Something about worshipping his muse?"

"Oh." She covered her smile and giggled. "Now what?"

"I think you should stay next to him and continue with the attention."

"Is that a good id—"

Fabian held up a finger to cut her off. "Maybe it's something that's been missing from his life longer than one girlfriend. You've obviously had quite the effect on him. Just sleep here tonight to help him work through this. You know it's fine, and it's not as if I'm going anywhere, so I'll be here if anything else happens."

"So, you think he just needs to be held?"

"This is his aftercare," he shrugged. "Some of us want to be alone, some want to binge-watch, some want to go shopping—like moi—and some of us want to snuggle. We can't be sure what he really needs since he's not exactly conscious enough to tell us, so, we make do with what we know."

"I can do that." Gwen undid her boots and took them off before climbing into the bed next to Sebastian. She chewed on her lower lip. "Fab, he looked at me...."

"Like you were the entire world to him? Sounds like he's going to enjoy spending time at your feet. Once the two of you work of the kinks, anyway." Fabian snorted. "I am *not* sorry for that one!"

"Yeah, yeah. I'm more worried about whether he'll want to try again. Could be too much for him."

"Pfft, as if. Coddle your man and tell him he's cute, and he'll be fine when he wakes up. Maybe he'll even be more refreshed than usual." Fabian tucked a little of the blanket around her. "Good luck, babe. I'd love for it to work out. You deserve a break."

"Thanks, Fab." She waited for him to leave before slipping her arms under the blanket and hugging Sebastian. Gwen thought he was still asleep at first, but his blue eyes popped open as she got comfortable.

"I fell asleep. I'm so sorry."

"It's ok. You're obviously tired."

"Are you going to stay with me?"

"Of course."

"I was worried you might leave. What happened? Why are we lying down?"

"I'll explain later, but for now just know I'm with you, and I'm not going to let you fall. You can go back to sleep."

"Your heart..." Sebastian shifted so he was half-lying on Gwen with his head on her chest and her arms still circling him.

"I'm sorry," she said quietly.

"For what?"

"You're inexperienced, and I should have been more mindful. I wasn't expecting you to drop like that."

"I consented, and I don't think either of us could have predicted what would happen. It's not your fault. Maybe I've just gotten used to being dismissed, but this is perfect and exactly what I need." He yawned and let his eyes close again.

"You were wasted on your ex."

"Maybe. Doesn't matter. I'm here now. Is it all right if I go back to sleep? I can't believe how tired I am."

"Of course, and when you wake up, we can talk about what happened and see if you still want to take me out for that coffee."

"Mm. Yeah nah, I don't want to do that anymore."

"Oh." Gwen tried to keep the sudden sting of hurt from her voice. "That's...I understand."

"I don't want to go for coffee. I want to cook dinner for you and feed you your favorite candies while you relax on the couch and watch a movie. Maybe you'll let me rub your feet, too? Wearing those boots has to be hard on them. And we can do anything else you want. I just want to cook dinner for you and rub your feet."

"I see." Gwen couldn't help her smile. "Well, my good boy, we can talk about it when you're more yourself again." She made sure he was completely asleep before drifting off herself. *What a strange night.* "You might actually make a great sub, Sebastian. Good night."

2

Consent

January 16th

Gwen swirled her tea and resisted the urge to check the time. *He's not late, I'm just early. Remember, this is just a casual meeting where we discuss what happened at the club and decide if we want to try this.* She glanced around the café, fingers tapping against the heavy paper cup in her hands. *What am I doing? This probably won't work out, just like last time and the time before that.*

"Uh-m." Sebastian walked up to her table in black slacks and a slate grey wool coat. He smoothed his short, dark blond hair back nervously. "Hi. May I sit?"

"Please."

"I'm not late, am I? One of my neighbors stopped me on my way out and wanted to chat." He shrugged off his coat and draped it over the wooden chair before pulling it out. They both grimaced as the legs scraped across the tile. "Sorry."

"No worries, you're on time. I'm usually a little early." She clasped her hands on the table in front of her. "So, Sebastian, I gave you a week to process and think things over with the option to take longer if necessary. Are you sure you're ready to talk about this after only three days?"

"Absolutely."

"Good. I'm sure you're full of questions, but let's start simple. How are you?"

"Great, actually. Ever since the, uh, the other night," he blushed, "I've been so.... I haven't been this relaxed in forever, and I've actually slept better the last couple of nights. What about you?"

"I'm good."

"I would also like to apologize."

"For what?"

"For how I acted. I don't know what came over me, and I got pushy when you were just trying to be responsible and keep me from doing anything I might've regretted. Thank you for not taking advantage of me and trying to protect me from my idiot self. What... what happened to me?"

"Before we get into that, do you want a coffee or something?" *He looks worried.* "We might be here for a little while. Considering the topic, we may want to have this conversation somewhere with more privacy."

"Where did you have in mind? I'm assuming you want to keep it somewhere neutral still."

"We could go back to the club. It would be quiet there now, and Fabian would let us use the office."

"You two seem very close."

"Is that a hint of jealousy I hear?" Gwen's lips slipped into any easy, teasing smile.

"I'm not jealous," Sebastian lied, "but it'd be nice to know if there's anything between you. I'm serious about being monogamous."

"Well," she sipped her tea, "Fab is a long-time friend, and I've been a VIP member of the club since it was a random idea that popped out of his mouth. We met at university and became friends instantly. I was there when he met his partner, John—they were wonderful together. The Collared Heart was their baby, but John didn't get to see it happen, so, I took over his part in bringing it to fruition. Think of me as the silent partner in the club."

"You invested in it?"

"Time, energy, love. A little money I suppose, but not any huge amount, just enough to help get the idea off the ground. The biggest way I invested was being there for Fabian. We painted, refurbished the stage and bar, and put in some hundred thousand little touches most people don't even notice." Gwen let out a little laugh. "If you're ever on stage, there's a…well, maybe I'll show you some time, but to give you a blunt answer, there's nothing more than friendship there. We've played together a few times, but it's been quite a while."

"That's fair and thank you for being upfront."

"I'm serious about being monogamous, too. It's a deal-breaker for me, and I say that as someone who's tried being part of a polycule before."

"What about multiple…um," he glanced around and leaned in, "submissives?"

"That I've done in more of a learning and stage setting, but in my personal life, I prefer to only have one. It's just, you know, too much for my brain to handle. I need to focus on one person."

Sebastian nodded thoughtfully. "So, what are your goals as a Domme then? Or, I guess, why are you a Domme? What does it mean to you?" Clouds scudded across the sun, causing the light playing across her face to darken. She seemed closed off. "Should I not have asked that?"

"No, it's an appropriate question to ask, but the long answer is complicated. Would it be all right if I gave you a simpler one for now? Until we know each other better?"

"Of course."

She chewed on her bottom lip, trying to decide how best to put it into words. "I've always been a giver. I want my partner to be happy, but I've always ended up sacrificing my happiness to make that happen. Me being a Domme, my goal, is to make sure that transfer of power, attention, affection…emotion…doesn't go one way in my partnerships. You should enjoy what we do just as much as I do, and vice versa."

"Are there ever instances where that isn't the case?"

"Sure. I mean, there's always going to be compromise and collaboration in partnerships. You may want to try something I'm not into, and as long as it isn't a limit for me, I'll probably be willing to try." She gulped down the rest of her tea. "Do you, uh, want something to drink?" Mouth dry and nerves starting to get the better of her, Gwen popped out of her chair.

"Allow me. Please." Sebastian rose somewhat more gracefully and took her empty cup. "Would you like more tea or something else?"

"Coffee. Black." She sat down again and watched Sebastian get in line. "Mm." *Nice view from behind, too.* The lunch crowd began to clear out of the café, and by the time he returned with two coffees, Gwen's anxiety had calmed. "Thank you."

"Of course." Sebastian set the drinks down and opened his mouth to say something but stopped. While waiting, he'd spent the time collecting his thoughts and deciding how to proceed. What should he ask next? What was off the table until they knew each other better? How fast was too fast? "You're not as...bossy as I was expecting. Pushy, I guess, would be a better word."

"Pushing people from the start doesn't exactly instill trust. If we did play together, I might try to push you to your limits, within reason, but only if you want me to."

"I don't like pain," he blurted.

"Me neither." One corner of her mouth twitched in a wry smile. "I don't enjoy inflicting pain."

"Not even spanking?"

"You're kind of fixated on that for someone who isn't into it."

"Well, I noticed you checking me out while I was in line."

Busted. She blushed and shrugged. "Maybe. You *are* nice to look at, but I still wouldn't spank you unless you asked me to."

"Hm." He tucked that curiosity away for later. "Still, I'm pleasantly surprised by all of this. You're not at all what I expected. You're so...chill."

Gwen snorted. "I've been called many things, but chill has never been one of them."

"But you are. I mean, I'm presuming you're nervous, too, so maybe 'chill' isn't the best word. Maybe...I can't think of the right one, but unaggressive and accessible. Like, you're not—like, I know you're not going tell me everything right now, and maybe not ever, but we can still have an open conversation, and I don't feel, you know...." He shrugged.

"Pressured?"

"Mhm."

"Being," she paused as another patron walked by, "what I am means, to me, being responsible and making sure potential, uh, partners feel safe enough with me to be vulnerable. I have to feel that way, too, about them, and no one gets there by being forceful."

"Mm. Yeah." Sebastian sipped his coffee thoughtfully. "If I wanted to move forward with…e-exploring this and perhaps continue getting to know more about each other, what would, uh, what would you say to that?"

"Really?"

"Really."

Gwen wiggled unconsciously in her seat. "Yeah, ok."

"Is that a happy dance?"

"No," she said, blushing furiously.

He thought better of teasing her. "Do you have any free time today? I'd like to take you to dinner."

"Oh? Is there something specific you're wanting to *Thai* out?"

"Hah." Sebastian clasped his hands and put his elbows on the table, grinning. "I am in *so* much trouble."

3

Obedience

April 19th

The Collared Heart been loud and crowded, full of bodies taut with anticipation and need, everyone seeking their own form of fulfillment. Somehow, they found each other in all the noise, just two people adrift in a sea of tension. Months of casual meets for coffee and lunch led them here, and now that they were finally ready to go, Gwen's heart threatened to jump out of her chest. Tonight, she stood in Sebastian's Manhattan loft, watching him lean against the kitchen island, and she swore the muted city noises below were louder than anything the club could conjure. *What if I mess up? This could ruin everything we've built so far.*

"Gingerbread." His voice was quiet and bashful as the word tripped out of his mouth.

"Seriously?" She raised her eyebrows and grinned, nerves starting to calm in the face of how absurdly appropriate the word was. It sounded even cuter with his accent.

"Sure. I never cared for the stuff, and the word's always sounded odd to me. I doubt I'm going to yell it out accidentally if I get too excited."

"You're adorable," she said with an appreciative sigh as her eyes darted over all 6-foot-2 of him. Under the plain black t-shirt and jeans, she could tell Sebastian worked out regularly. He kept his dark blond beard trimmed short, so it highlighted the angles of his jaw rather than disguising them. She loved the little scar on his chin. Intrigued sea-blue eyes watched her from beneath a mess of wavy hair. *He's let his hair get past his ears. Good, I'll have something to wrap my fingers in.* "I doubt I could keep a straight face if you said that, and I certainly won't mistake it for encouragement. It'll work. For tonight, at least. Don't forget it though. If anything goes wrong or you're uncomfortable at any time, that's your cue to me to stop."

"And if I do? Since we've not done this before, I might, you know…."

"Color system. That's the best fall back. Yellow for pause, red for stop."

"Green for go. I understand." He smirked as she moved around the table to set a black bag on the counter. It unrolled to reveal a collection of rope, shears, and other goodies. A 'rope kit' he remembered her calling it. Sebastian wanted to look through it, but instead he watched her fiddle with everything, debating where she wanted to start. This was their first true session together and only his second time allowing someone else to be in control. Part of him wondered if he could go through with it. Gwen was certainly the type of woman he preferred, with a devious smile and sharp mind, and he'd always wanted to try letting go. *But can I? Wanting to doesn't mean I can. This could be a total disappointment for her. I could be a disappointment.* One thing they'd discussed in their meetings was Sebastian's lifelong need to be involved in every part of whatever he was working on. He couldn't bring himself to delegate to anyone, not even his brother, whom he trusted more than anyone. Gwen offered an opportunity to explore another side of himself he rarely showed. As they'd taken the time to learn a bit more about each other, Sebastian began to open up, and they became cautiously hopeful the arrangement might work out. "I do have another question."

"Yes?"

"How far can we go?"

"As in?" She tilted her head slightly and nodded once, inviting him to continue.

"I like you, Gwen. A lot. You're intelligent and funny and so beautiful, and I've been dying to kiss you. I don't want to rush. I'm just putting it out there and hoping you, um, feel the same, and if…if things get heated tonight—and if you're willing—maybe we could…."

"Since this is our first time, I think we need to tread carefully. If we get to that point and decide we're both comfortable with moving forward, then we can explore more options, but first steps first."

"What if I want to tell you I'm comfortable and want more? Do we have a word or something for that?" His fingers itched to touch her right then, to run them through her dark hair down to her hips so he could pull her body against his and kiss her. Normally, that's what he would be doing by now. Sebastian's hands stayed in his pockets and his eyes on hers, just as she'd told him to when they started preparing for this night, although it took all his will power. *If that's how she dresses for work, I'm going to be in trouble the nights she has time to go home and change first.* He held in a groan as his eyes lingered over the curve of her waist and hips sharply accentuated in a black pencil skirt.

"I don't see why we can't have something just in case," Gwen said after a thoughtful pause.

"I'm listening."

"Oh? You mean you don't have another food you want to use? Maybe something you absolutely love?"

"No," he said with a small laugh. "Do you have anything you normally use?"

"I've not had a submissive I've been that intimate with, and bondage doesn't always involve sex."

"That doesn't mean you don't have something in mind." *Sometimes it's hard to get a direct answer.* Like him, Gwen's needs and desires had always been second place, making it hard to say what she wanted even when she was free to do so. From his research, Sebastian learned even dominants could be shy at first and needed encouragement. *I'm submitting to her, not leading. How can I phrase it better?* "Tell me what you want me to say. Please."

"'Ymroddi.' It means to surrender, to devote, or to yield." Gwen motioned him toward the chair he'd set out in the empty space between the door and the back of his couch.

"Em-roth…eh? What language is that?"

"Welsh, and it's 'em-roh-thee'."

"You speak Welsh?"

"Some. My grandparents were Welsh immigrants, and I spent a

lot of time with them growing up, so they taught me."

"You're amazing. I mean it," he said when she made a face expressing her disagreement. "You choose to take charge of your life rather than passively waiting for it to happen. You see something you're interested in, and if you're able to pursue it, you at least try. That's more than most. I admire that—respect it."

"Flattery won't stop me from tying you up."

"I certainly hope not." Sebastian grinned, but there were little butterflies in his stomach as he went to the chair he'd set up. *This is happening.*

"I might even be tempted to gag you if you start to sound insincere," she said, grabbing a few lengths of deep blue nylon rope and a blindfold from the bag rolled out across the butcher-block countertop.

"But then I won't be able to say 'gingerbread' or 'ehm-roh-the'." He tried to sound out the unfamiliar word.

"Better." Her heels clicked across the hardwood as she approached, rope in hand.

"I don't see a gag in there anyway."

"I promise you I can improvise if the need arises. And you consent. Shall we begin?"

"Please, Mistress."

"'Mistress'?"

"Not quite it?"

"No. I think...hm. I'm not sure what I want, but 'Mistress' doesn't sit right."

"What about 'my Lady'?" Sebastian watched her lips twitch into a smile. During their talks, he learned Gwen wanted to be respected by her partner, instead of mocked as some of her boyfriends had done. *Maybe 'Mistress' sounds patronizing to her.* "Please...my Lady."

"Then take your shirt off." Pearly, jagged scars covered part of his right side and forearm. *Ouch. What caused those? Must have been painful.* The chair he'd picked for their session was armless and padded in a slate-grey polyester. Gwen wondered how long it would take him to realize it was a bad choice. The wide, high back wasn't going to be as comfortable as he thought, but he'd insisted it would be fine. "And what shall I call you? 'My pet?' No." Gwen walked around him, lips pursed in thought. "How about 'my Knight'?"

"You're my Lady and I'm your Knight? Do ladies typically hold knights captive?"

"I suppose not. Does it matter?"

"It does to me. I want you to be pleased. Dragons hold knights and ladies captive. Perhaps I should call you 'my Dragoness' instead? Or maybe 'my Queen' is better?"

"You're treading dangerously close to calling me your Goddess again."

"Would that be a problem?"

"Mm." Gwen bit her lip and said the title in her head. *Would it be a problem?* They were still just testing the waters for now, and they could always change it later. *But I do like the way it sounds.* "No, I don't think that will be a problem."

"My Goddess."

"So, would that make you my priest? My disciple?"

"I don't know. The idea of being your knight is appealing—protecting you, worshipping you, carrying out your commands. I can do anything you desire."

"All right, my Knight. Are you ready?"

"Yes, my Goddess."

"Are you sure you want me to blindfold you?" Gwen dangled the blindfold between them.

"Yes." He sat with his hands in his lap and watched her slip off her peacock-blue pumps. "You love that color I take it."

"I do, now hush."

"Yes, Goddess," Sebastian said with a little smirk. As she slipped the satin over his eyes, he realized there were no gaps to let light in and his smile faltered. He was completely blind. "I'm ok," he said when he felt her hesitate. The strap tightened until it was snug.

Gwen's touch was light but firm as she guided first one arm and then the other behind the chair. She made sure they were at a comfortable angle and started with a simple, single-column tie to bring his wrists together. She anchored it to the legs of the chair before stepping away for another length of rope. Each touch was careful, reassuring, both making sure he was all right and letting him know she was there. His shoes came off and Gwen nudged his knees apart so she could tie his calves to the chair.

When she moved away again, there was something different

about it. The five seconds it took her to walk to the counter seemed five hours to Sebastian, and he felt deprived, alone, and helpless. He trembled a little when she touched him again and the tension drained away.

"I've got you."

"Mhm," he mumbled. Sebastian didn't realize he'd been holding his breath until it came out in one big exhale. The next set of knots went from his wrists, across the tops of his thighs, and just below his knees to meet the knots around his calves. *I can't move at all.* He tested the rope around his wrists. When it didn't budge, panic swirled around his mind. He couldn't see or touch Gwen, only listen and wait. The part of his brain accustomed to being in control demanded to know what he was doing. *She's so close. If my hands were free, I could just reach out and hold her.* Sebastian sensed her working over each knot, checking to make sure nothing was too tight. A few loose strands of hair fell across his face, tickling his nose, but the scent of wisteria and jasmine distracted him. *I want to touch her. I need to.* His body tensed at the vacuum when she stepped away again. "Um…Goddess."

"Yes?"

"I…." He didn't know how to ask for what he wanted. "Y-yellow?"

"Are you all right?"

"Nah yeah, I just…don't leave me?"

"I'm not going to leave you. I'm right here."

"I know, and I can hear you, but when you move away, I…."

"Ah." Gwen remembered being tied up by an ex once when she was still new to the scene. Once. He knew she hated being restrained and didn't want to do it, but he convinced her she would try it if she "really loved" him. Then he used her fear against her and left her bound, blinded, and gagged in the room by herself for what felt like an eternity. When he finally came back, he laughed off her anger and panic and said she was being over-dramatic. That was the end of the relationship, and it was almost the end of her interest in kink. So, she understood how isolating and agonizing it could be when you couldn't move or see anything, experienced or not. "Is there something you want me to do when I need to step away?"

"Can you just…."

"Do you want me to stop?"

"No, I just want you to stay. Here." He swallowed hard. Having to ask for what he wanted, to voice it, was difficult, especially when he wasn't sure how to articulate it in the first place. Sebastian still wasn't sure if it was all right to ask for something when he was the submissive or how much was too much.

"The more feedback you can give me, the better. I need to know when something is bothering you or if there's something else you would prefer. You're uncomfortable with me stepping away, so if we decide to do this again, I'll make sure to keep everything close enough I don't need to. Would you rather I took the blindfold off?"

"No," he admitted. The blindfold and rope were pleasant torture, and Sebastian didn't want her to take any of it off, he just didn't want to be alone. "Will you please stay right here with me? Even if it means no more knots or whatever tonight, I just need for you to be touching me."

"All right. But you forgot something," Gwen said, teasing just a little. Thankfully, she'd already grabbed the last couple of things she wanted, and they were within easy reach on a decorative table next to them. If it were big enough, she would've used it instead of the counter for her bag.

"Please?"

"Ask me properly if you want to continue. I need your clear consent."

"Oh, right, sorry." His anxiety was clouding his thoughts, so he pushed it aside, focusing on the sensation of her hand hovering over his head. "Please, don't stop touching me. Don't leave me alone, my Goddess. And, um, green."

"Ok, I promise to stay right here with you, my Knight." Gwen smiled and ran her fingers through his short hair. Sebastian relaxed visibly at the contact. She checked his hands and feet again before slipping on a set of silver claws. "I'll take very good care of you," she said tracing one finger in a slow line down his sternum.

The sensation of claws wasn't painful, but it was surprising. Sebastian gasped, skin prickling as his body tensed. It was teasing without release, and he started squirming at his inability to do anything. Just as anxiety worked its way back in and the need to touch her was overwhelming, as the word was about to cross his lips, Gwen ran her claws along his collarbone and up his neck, sending shivers all over his body. Her thumb caressed his jaw, and she asked one, simple question: did he want her to stop. Sebastian's entire mindset shifted. "No." He wasn't sure if it was stubbornness, determination to finish what he'd started, real enjoyment, or a combination of all three, but he didn't want her to stop. Sebastian wanted her to be in control. He craved more. "Ymroddi." Although he couldn't see her, he knew she was smiling by the way her lips curved against his skin as they followed the trail left by her fingers.

Gwen didn't quite know what to think of the situation. Even if he wanted to take things further, she needed to be sure of his limits. She left blue lip-prints in the wake of her claws and loved the way his skin prickled. When she reached his ear, she nibbled the lobe and flicked her tongue over the soft flesh. *I did say we could explore more options if we want the same things. And he's so sexy all tied up and eager for more.* "What would you like to negotiate for, my Knight?"

"Kiss me. Tease me. I guess…if we're more comfortable after that for a bit, we can renegotiate. I crave more of you." Sebastian swallowed hard as Gwen laughed, her breath rushing over his sensitive ear. *Maybe I shouldn't have worn jeans.*

"I can agree to that." Gwen's eyes wandered to his lips. *How many times have I wanted to kiss him during our dates? And knowing he's been wanting the same thing….* "Any particular way you want to be teased?"

"I leave myself in your capable hands, my Goddess."

"I see. And you remember your safe word? What is it?"

"If I say it now, then our session will be over, and I'm not ready for that. I promise to say it if I need to."

"Good boy, you're paying attention." Gwen smirked and started thinking of other ways she might tease him.

"I…I…um." He cleared his throat and blushed.

"You're stuttering again. Did you like me calling a 'good boy?'"

"Yeah," he mumbled. Sebastian's body hummed with excitement. *I can't believe that one little compliment has me so flustered.* "Please proceed at your pleasure." All he heard was a zipper and the rustling of fabric. The scent of her perfume wafted over him as she circled around to recheck each knot. The next moment was a rush of information his brain had trouble processing all at once. The soft sound of clothing falling to the floor. Gwen's hands on his shoulders as her knees slid along the outside of his legs until she sat in his lap, her body pressing against his bare chest. The most he could be sure of was she wore some lacy underwire with panties he assumed matched—because he knew by now she wanted her things to match. *Are they blue like her shoes? She's so warm.* He could just barely feel the silk of her stockings on his forearms. All of that wove together with her lotion and shampoo to create a nice image in his mind of how she looked sitting on top of him. When her mouth met his and she slid her tongue in to tease him, he moaned at the taste of chocolate and blackberries. Gwen's hands were split between keeping his head where she wanted it and running her claws across his skin. A whimper escaped Sebastian as her claws disappeared and she scooted back to perch on his knees; he drew in a sharp breath when the claws trailed up the inside of his thigh.

"Do you need me?" She wanted to sound calm and in control, but her racing heart made the question come out breathless. *He is scrumptious. I'm glad he took his shirt off.* "Do you need your Goddess?"

"Yes."

"Tell me what you want." Delicate claws traced circles on the inside of his thigh.

"You." He shuddered.

"I need you to say it clearly. On your own."

"I want," he swallowed hard, "I—" Sebastian's phone chimed somewhere in the background of the blood pounding in his ears.

"You didn't silence your phone?"

"Ah." He tried to remember. *Who would be calling? I told everyone I'm busy tonight.* "I swear I put it on silent."

"Whose ring tone is that?"

"Um." Sebastian tilted his head and bit back the dread forming in his stomach. "That's my ex." The phone continued to ring in the long pause that followed.

"And do you want to speak with your ex?"

"No. I told her to stop calling me," he said with an aggravated sigh.

"It's been almost a year. Why don't you block her?" Gwen ran her claws back up his chest while the phone rang again.

"I did, but she got a new number and started up again. I planned to change mine, but I kept putting it off and then I met you. I was afraid it'd be weird if I changed it right after we start talking." The phone went silent.

"I'm going to step away and turn your ringer off. When I come back, we'll decide if we can continue tonight." Gwen didn't take her time exactly, but she took a few extra seconds to recompose herself as she picked his phone up from the coffee table and silenced it. Jealousy wasn't an emotion she normally wrestled with, yet the idea of this woman calling made her bristle. *Maybe it's because we're getting to a good part? We're not officially a.... We're not partners or in a relationship. He doesn't belong to me, and he's been very clear things are over between them. But tonight...for tonight Sebastian is* mine. She interlaced her fingers to keep from rubbing her hands together and licked her lips anxiously. *Stop it. One deep inhale. One deep exhale. Deep in. Deep out.*

"Are you angry?" Sebastian sensed his Goddess standing in front of him again and turned his face into her hand when she stroked his cheek.

"I just," she paused to take a deep breath, "I'm not interested in sharing. If you're mine, you can't belong to anyone else. Which probably sounds ridiculous since I'm not asking to be your girlfriend, but that's what I need."

"I can agree to that, so long as you don't have anyone else either." The silence was deafening.

"Well, then." Gwen leaned in, hair brushing against his chest as she kissed his neck. "We have an agreement. Mutual exclusivity. And you're getting a new number *and* a new phone. Your screen is cracked next to your volume buttons, like you tried to mute it too hard."

"That's very probable." Sebastian nuzzled her wrist. "May we continue, my Goddess?" Her answer was to run both hands down his chest and along the inside of his thighs. Sebastian grunted and shuddered.

"You were about to tell me what you want."

"Was I? I can't remember. Will you be so kind as to help me find the words?"

"Are you sassing me?"

"Now, why would I do that?"

"Hm. Maybe you don't want to keep going?" Gwen brushed her lips against his while her claws went back to tracing little circles through his jeans.

"Don't stop. Please."

"Then tell me what you want."

"I want you." He regretted leaving his pants on as she teased him to the point of throbbing.

"Go on." Her hands disappeared but she nibbled his ear, inviting him to speak. "Tell me."

"I want you to take all of me. I won't hold anything back." Sebastian felt her hands on his knees.

"Be more specific." She flicked her tongue along his neck.

"Honestly?"

"Always."

"I've wanted you since I first saw you, and not because of those sexy leather boots or the corset. Everything about you draws me in. I *need* you."

"Like a drug?"

"Like air. Without you, there's none in the room, and it's like I'm suffocating. Let me breathe, Goddess."

"Ask me for what you want."

"Will you please let me breathe? Will you take me for yourself?"

"All?" She dropped her bra next to the chair and slipped her panties off.

"Yes, I," he cleared his throat nervously, not used to asking, "I want to feel you, be inside of you while you take what you want from me. And will you, um, let me come tonight?" Sebastian bit his lip, heat rushing to his cheeks again. Her breath was warm on his skin and sent shivers over his body. *Please don't change your mind about this.*

"I want to hear you say it again." Gwen sat back down on his lap, hands moving to the top of his jeans and tugging the zipper down. One claw-less hand reached in to stroke him, and she smiled at how much he wanted her.

"I surrender to you, Goddess. Ymroddi." Sebastian gasped and moaned when she slid onto his erection and thought she may have gasped, too. All he knew for sure was it felt good to be inside of Gwen while she gripped the back of the chair and thrust her hips against his. *I don't feel lace anymore.* She pressed her bare breasts against his chest, and he instinctively tried to wrap his hands around her waist as he came close to climaxing. *Man, she's great with rope. These knots aren't budging.*

"Not yet." She slowed the pace

"Please."

"Not yet." Gwen waited until his breathing steadied before beginning again. When she orgasmed, she whispered "not yet." She drove him close to the edge several times, only to pull him back, and when she came a second time, he obediently restrained himself.

"Please, Goddess," he begged. Sebastian panted as she tightened around him again, driving him wild with the intensity. *"Please*, may I come?"

"Yes. Come for me, my Knight." She wrapped one hand around the back of his neck and kissed him while they came.

Everything slowed. Their movement. Their breathing. Theirs hearts. Sebastian buried his face in her neck and waited for his body to stop trembling. "W...wow."

Gwen giggled and kissed him again. "Good boy. How do you feel?"

"Amazing. Thank you. Are you...?"

"I'm pretty amazing myself."

"Yeah, you are." Sebastian flexed his fingers. "What happens now?"

"I untie you and make sure you're all right."

"Would it be okay if we laid down for a little while?"

"Of course." Gwen pulled away and undid the knots more quickly than she tied them, checking his hands and feet as she went. She made sure the only light came from his bedside lamp before she removed the blindfold. "Wait a few minutes before you stand." She massaged his wrists and hands and gave him a glass of water.

"They do match," he said, noticing her bra and panties on the floor.

"Come on." Gwen rolled her eyes and helped him to the bed. "You might be weak for a little bit."

"Will you stay?"

"I said I'd lie down with you." She pulled his jeans off completely and tucked the sheet around him.

"No, I mean will you *stay*? For the night? Or do you have to leave?" Sebastian grabbed her hand as she finished settling him. When he opened one eye, her expression was hesitant. "If you have to leave it's ok, it would just be nice if you stayed."

"I can...but I didn't bring an overnight bag, so I'll need to borrow a shirt."

"I'd love nothing more." Part of him flinched when she walked away, so he kept his eyes open to reassure himself she was still there. "Second drawer on the left." He watched her slip one of his black-t-shirts on before going to clean up. "Do you need any help?"

"No, I need for you to stay over there and keep drinking that water. And don't sit up too fast," she added as he did just that. Her lips twitched into a smile. "I've got this."

"Yes, Goddess." He rubbed his face and sipped dutifully.

"You know, when we're not playing, you don't have to call me that." Gwen coiled the different lengths of rope and tucked them away with the shears and her claws.

"What if I want to? When it's just us? I love calling you my 'Goddess' and my muse."

"Do you have any poetry for me tonight, my sweet Sebastian?"

"You *are* poetry."

"Flatterer." Clothes folded neatly over the back of the couch, she joined him on the bed and checked him over again. "Any numbness or tingling?"

"Nah."

"Any dizziness?"

"Only when I sat up too fast."

"How are you otherwise?"

"Aside from my thoughts being mush and my body floating, I'm just super tired and clingy. I'm not normally clingy."

"Everyone's different." Gwen smoothed away his frown and tried not to laugh. "Do you want me to turn the light off?"

"Please." Sebastian took his arm away from his eyes once it was dark and set the glass on the nightstand. "Big spoon or little?"

"Hm?" She stretched out alongside him, one hand on his leg.

"Do you prefer being the big spoon or the little spoon?"

"How about neither right now?" Gwen rolled onto her side, putting her hand on his chest and one leg across him.

"Okay," he said, grinning in the dark. Sebastian slipped one arm under her so she could rest her head on his shoulder.

Gwen let out a slight hiss when his other hand settled onto her ribs. "Could you shift your hand a bit. My ribs are...sensitive."

"I'm sorry. Is everything ok? It sounded like—did I hurt you?"

"It's not anything you did. Someone I used to date broke my ribs—among other things—a couple of times. They've been a little sensitive ever since. Maybe it's just in my head, but they still hurt sometimes."

"Both sides?"

"No, mostly just the left."

He remained quiet for a few minutes, chewing over the information. "I know I can't fix it or make it better. I'm grateful you've told me, and I'll do my best to be careful, so I don't cause you any pain. Please, let me know if something hurts or bothers you."

"Of course." After a moment, she kissed his cheek and murmured, "you're very sweet."

Sebastian couldn't think of anything to say and since the topic seemed to be over, he steered his thoughts back to all he'd experienced that night. "You were right."

"About?"

"The chair. Long-term, it's not very comfortable."

Gwen snorted. "Experience has its benefits."

"I'll get a different one for next time." He felt her cheek move against his shoulder as she nodded.

"I can give you some guidance if you're open to it, but please try to pick something besides grey or white. You need some color in here."

"As you wish, my Goddess." Sebastian turned to face her and carefully wrapped his other arm around her waist. Just as he was almost lulled to sleep by the scent of wisteria and jasmine, an idea popped into his head. "Oh, I thought of something!"

"Hm?"

"I'll get two chairs. My Goddess needs a comfortable throne to sit on while I'm at her feet. Maybe in her favorite color?"

"That would be lovely," she mumbled. "Now, go to sleep."

"Hey?"

"Hm?"

"Did I do all right?"

"Yes, you did very well, my Knight."

4

Changes

July 23rd

Sebastian's hand trembled slightly as he hit send. *Will Gwen still come?* Despite keeping things quiet, his brother had managed to figure out he was seeing someone new, but the real nature of their relationship still seemed to be a secret. Nate wasted no time trying to find a way to meet the woman who'd finally gotten Sebastian to relax, and when the excuses didn't stop, he'd taken it upon himself to make the meeting happen. Friday remained Sebastian's usual play night with Gwen, and he'd been setting up when his brother arrived. Unannounced and bearing beer. *Pain in my ass.*

"So? Do I get to meet her? When will she get here?" Nate slouched in the middle of the couch and stretched his legs out.

"I don't know. She hasn't texted me back yet." *This could go terribly. Or it could go very well. Either way, I'm not sure I'm ready for it.* Sebastian noticed Nate was getting overly comfortable on the couch. "Put your feet on my table, and I'll lay you flat, Plan B."

"Calm down, Broken Condom."

"Go suck on a lollie, ya Ocker."

"Fuckin' Wowser. You're no fun sometimes."

Sebastian started to retort but someone knocked, so he settled for flipping him off. *That was awfully quick.* He knew it took longer than an hour for Gwen to go from work to home, shower, get ready, and arrive at his place. *She could've already been on the way here, but that should still take a bit.* He offered many times for her to leave some things at his place to make it easier, but she'd only agreed to keep a few toiletries and a single change of clothes. "Hey, gorge—"

"Hi, Sweetie!"

"Mum?" Sebastian hugged the short, grey-haired woman in shock and glared at his brother. "Tell me you didn't."

"Hey, Mum." Nate grinned and popped up from the couch to greet their mother. "I'm glad you made it."

"Well, I couldn't miss the chance to meet your brother's new girlfriend. I mean, you changed your number and everything, Sebastian! She's had quite the impact on you."

"Mhm." Sebastian hung his mom's jacket on the wall and tried to count how many ways he might be mortified tonight.

"Here." She handed him a glass pan covered in foil. "I brought a little taste of home—vanilla slice. Nathaniel said she likes blackberries, so I added made the topping blackberry and tossed a few into the chocolate custard. I guess that means it's chocolate slice instead!" She laughed and patted him on the shoulder. Normally, she made a vanilla custard sandwiched between layers of puff pastry topped with strawberry icing—only deviating when her boys asked for something special. She looked around the open space and took in the changes in her oldest son's décor. "Oh."

"Oh?" Sebastian pulled his attention away from investigating the new take on his favorite childhood dessert. *I know that tone. And how does Nate know about the blackberries?*

"This must be Gwen's." She walked over to a wing-backed chair and ran her hand over the peacock-blue, satin brocade. Curved ebony legs in a Victorian style supported the very plush seat. "You bought a chair just for her. It's very lovely."

"Yeah, well, she told me I need more color in here, so I picked up a couple of things. I thought the chair would be a nice idea, especially since she loves to read." *And she sometimes uses me as a footstool.*

"I see."

"Mum?"

"Hm? Oh, it's nothing, I'm just eager to meet her. Will any of her family be joining us?"

"Honestly, I didn't know either of you were coming over. If I had, I might've been more prepared." He glared at Nate again as soon as their mom turned her back. "A warning would have been nice."

"Not to worry, it'll happen eventually. Where's dinner? I don't smell anything cooking."

"We were planning to order out." His phone let out a soft, musical sound—Gwen was on her way. If he wasn't comfortable with her meeting his brother, he just had to say the word. Sebastian made an annoyed face and texted a quick reply that he was looking forward to his Goddess meeting Nate but hoped she didn't mind his mother had been invited. The typing icon appeared and disappeared a few times before her reply came through. *Order whatever mum chooses? I hope she doesn't insist on cooking.* "What sounds good to eat tonight, Mum?"

"You know I'm not picky, Sweetie. Whatever you two were going to get is fine."

"Gwen said to order whatever you choose."

"Ah, so she didn't find an excuse not to come then. Or did you tell her she had to?" Nate smirked a little too knowingly over his beer.

"She makes the decisions, Nate. I wouldn't dream of telling her what to do." Sebastian smiled charmingly as his brother choked on his beer.

"I'm going to borrow your toilet real quick. Oh, and maybe we could get some Thai."

"I'll see if I have a menu," As soon as the bathroom door shut, Sebastian turned on his brother. "The hell, Nate? Not only did *you* show up without warning on the night I keep just for Gwen, but you invited *Mum?*"

"She was so excited when she found out, I couldn't *not* invite her."

"You could have *not* invited yourself and then it wouldn't have been an issue. This is *my* place. You can't just—ugh. I hate it when you go through my things." Sebastian threw up his hands.

"To be fair, you shouldn't leave your planner on your desk for the world to see."

"People don't normally snoop around my office. Damn stickybeak, what else?"

"What else what?" Nate looked at him innocently.

"What else have you been going through? Mum might've missed your meaning, but I didn't."

"It's not my fault you left your online wish list up." He shrugged the question off.

"I didn't," Sebastian said. "I minimized the window."

"I needed to use the Internet." Nate waved his hand vaguely.

"Rubbish. You always open a new window."

"Fine, stubborn ass. Your birthday's coming up, and we needed ideas. You've given us *nothing*—no hints, no list, nothing."

"So, you saw…fuck." Sebastian buried his face in his hands. "Does Mum know?"

"Seriously? I wouldn't tell her that. But, Bash, shibari? Books on knots, Dom/sub dynamic, and ideas for 'play?' That's more than keeping things interesting in the bedroom." Nate shot his brother a questioning look.

"Gwen isn't my girlfriend, strictly speaking, but we're in an exclusive relationship. For as long as we're together, we don't see anyone else. Dating or otherwise."

"Frankly, I kind of figured you'd be the dominant one since you like being in control so much. But I guess I was wrong."

"I don't expect you to get it," Sebastian said defensively.

"Well, I don't have to." Nate clapped his brother on the shoulder. "You're more relaxed than I've seen you in years and obviously happy. If you'd been a little more upfront, I might not've preemptively told Mum you have a new girlfriend. You've always been open with me before. Did you not trust me enough to tell me about this?"

"It's not that."

"Did Gwen say you weren't allowed to talk about it?"

"No, she trusts my discretion. I just didn't know how to talk about it with you. How do you even start that conversation?" Sebastian shrugged.

"How did you even find your way into this relationship?" Nate leaned against the island and took a swig of his beer.

"Fair enough." Sebastian sighed and glanced toward the bathroom door. "You remember that club Mel is always going on about?"

"Sort of," he said after thinking about it for a minute.

"Apparently, it's a fetish club."

"And you went? Wow." Nate blinked and shook his head at the thought. "You're getting adventurous in your old age."

"He didn't tell me it was a fetish club," Sebastian replied, flipping Nate off at the same time. "His girlfriend dumped him, and he was upset, so he begged me to go with him. Mel claimed he didn't want to be standing around the club alone. Only, not thirty minutes after we arrived, he went off with some woman he'd never met and left me standing there alone." Sebastian rounded the island and rummaged through a drawer for the menus.

"You hate clubs, especially when you're by yourself. Why didn't you just leave?"

"I was going to, but I wanted to finish my drink, and I'm glad I didn't get the chance to leave. That's how I met Gwen." Sebastian heard the water in the bathroom. "Look, if you want all the details about how we met and got started, fine, but I'm not talking about it in front of mum."

"That conversation would be more awkward than when she decided it was time we knew about sex in the first place." Nate made a pained face.

"Oh my god, don't remind me."

"Don't remind you of what?" Their mom stepped out, brushing the front of her shirt, and smiling brightly

"Just some fond childhood memories Bash and I have." Nate chuckled and winked at his brother.

"You two were always such mischievous little rascals. All right. So. Thai?" She settled her arms on the island, mimicking Nate, and glanced from one to the other.

"Yeah." Sebastian passed her the menu and a notepad, and everyone scribbled down their order.

"What about Gwen?"

"Oh, it's all right, mum, I already know what she wants." He phoned in the order quickly and texted Gwen the ETA for dinner. "Great, looks like she'll be here about the same time dinner is."

"She doesn't live far then?"

"Far enough. I've offered to walk her over but she's an independent sort and won't hear of it."

"One day you might change her mind, Sweetie."

"I doubt that. If I could, she wouldn't be the woman I know." Sebastian faltered on the last part, prompting Nate to raise his eyebrows over their mother's head. "When she decides she's ready for me to pick her up, she'll tell me. Sometimes I feel blessed she permits me to carry anything or get the door for her." He discreetly stuck his tongue out when Nate rolled his eyes.

"'Blessed?' Hm doesn't 'Gwen' mean 'blessed' in Welsh?"

"Um, yeah, I think it does, as well as 'fair' and 'white.' I didn't know you knew any Welsh, Mum."

"I don't! It's just...." Her sons leaned closer, encouraging her to go on. "'Gwen' was one of the names I considered if I ever were to have a daughter." She ignored Nate, who covered his laugh with a cough.

"Y-you don't say. Well. Small world. Or something." Sebastian stuffed his hands in his pockets, then pulled them back out to gesture to the door. "You know, I just remembered, sometimes the Thai guy comes a little early, so I'm going to head downstairs and see if he's here yet."

"Great idea, Bash, we'll be waiting. Mum, you're not trying to hint-drop, are you? They practically just met," Nate chided her as the door closed.

Sebastian bolted down the stairs and stepped into the evening to wait. *This could be a long night.* The city air was sharpened by the scent of rain on hot as the day melted into a sticky summer night. *Count to ten. Breathe. Calm. Everything is going to be....* An image of his mother recounting some of his more embarrassing childhood moments to Gwen flashed in his mind. *Fuck.* He squeezed his eyes shut and visualized Gwen. The curve of her mouth when she thought of some way to tease him. Her fingers in his hair. Her waist. Her hips. Sebastian stood under the awning in front of his building, trying to keep his mind off his family. Someone stepped in front of him after a while and the scent of wisteria and jasmine push the city away as soft lips brushed against his neck. "My Goddess." He smiled and opened his eyes to see Gwen. "How are you this evening?"

"I'm all right. How is my Knight?"

"Better. I'm glad you came tonight." Instinctively, Sebastian tucked a wavy lock behind her ear before lifting her hand to his lips. "You are captivating." Her makeup was less dramatic than usual, and she'd left her hair loose, giving her a softer, more delicate appearance. *If only we could skip straight to the loving and cuddling. But first, my family.* "Now all we need is—"

"Hey, Mr. Sebastian! Got your food." A lanky teen walked up with a couple of bags in either hand.

"Oh, excellent timing." He fished his wallet out and paid the kid before taking the food.

"Thanks, man, have a great night!"

"You, too. Be careful," he said as the young man ran off. A few drops of rain spattered on the sidewalk. "Shall we head in?"

"Yes, and you can tell me what happened." Gwen walked into the building, blue heels clicking across the stone entry. Despite the mid-summer heat, she wore a long black skirt and a blue, long-sleeved blouse under a black bodice.

"I'm so sorry, Gwen, I left my planner open at work and Nate decided to go through it. Among other things. Can you—" He stopped when she held up one long finger.

"Hush. All right, so your brother saw we've been meeting regularly and made assumptions. He wanted to meet me, so he showed up on our night and then invited your mother. Right?"

"Right." Sebastian nodded, although she was focused on the steps in front of her rather than looking back at him. *She must've come straight from work.*

"Let's get through dinner, and we can talk about it later." Gwen tried to compose herself while they took the stairs to his fourth-floor apartment. Meet his brother? Sure, she supposed that was all right. Meet his mom? That she wasn't quite as ready for. Every time she'd taken that step, it normally spelled the end for whatever relationship she'd been in. *But this isn't a normal relationship*, she reminded herself. "Anything I should know before we go in?"

"My mum thinks you're my girlfriend, thanks to Nate, who thought the same initially. I didn't know what to do. Mum showed up right after I texted you about my brother." Sebastian huffed a little as he carried four people's worth of food.

"Are you sure you don't want help?"

"Positive. I've got it, Goddess." He shot her a cute smile meant to be encouraging but tripped up the stairs.

"My confidence is restored." Gwen snickered quietly while he righted himself. "Look, Bash, just tell her we've been seeing each other but it's not...." She shrugged.

"If my brother told her as much as I think he did, she knows we see each other regularly. And she saw your chair. To her, that's a huge step. Getting a new number was also big. All the changes I've made recently, and my improved disposition, are all positive and all because of you. She's eager to meet you."

"You said your brother thought I was your girlfriend 'initially?'"

"He may have snooped around in my online wish list and so had…ideas, and when he commented on the dynamic of our relationship, I corrected that impression. When mum wasn't in the room, I asked him to explain himself, and he told me about looking through the list because he was trying to get birthday ideas."

"I see." Gwen paused on the stairs and shrugged. "I suppose there's not much we can do about it now. So, on my way over I gave it some thought, and if you're up for it, we can still play subtly."

"Subtly?"

"Yeah, at least until we're alone. And we don't have to, of course, if you're not comfortable with it, but I won't ask for anything extreme."

"What did you have in mind?"

"So, here are the rules for tonight, should you choose to accept them." She resumed her ascent.

"The rules?"

"Did I stutter?"

"Ah, no, my Goddess, you did not."

"If, at any point, you wish for this to stop, you've only to say the word, and I can either come up with an excuse to leave or…."

"I'd actually rather you didn't leave. We can just stop whatever we're doing and…I don't know, but please, don't leave."

"All right." Even though it was an unexpected turn, she was happy Sebastian wanted her to stay. "During dinner, you'll need to follow some simple guidelines."

"You've been reading that book I got you," he said with a cheesy grin.

"Perhaps." She glanced over her shoulder at him with a heated look in her eyes and half a smirk. "While there's company, you may not refer to me as 'my Goddess', nor will I call you 'my Knight'. That would be, uh, odd—to say the least. You'll serve dinner to your mother and me."

"So far nothing unusual." Sebastian was expecting something a bit more elaborate, but they sounded like normal "meet the family" rules.

"You'll be well-mannered gentleman all night. This means pulling out my chair for me when I go to sit down, standing when I come to the table or get up to leave, filling my plate and glass, and asking if there's anything I need. You will excuse yourself after introducing me to your family and setting dinner down to change into the red t-shirt I bought you. I also expect you to go commando for the evening."

"C-commando?"

"Yes. And comb your hair the other way—the way I like it. Can you agree to those terms?"

"Mhm."

"One more thing. Whenever I say 'vanilla', I want you to imagine me naked until, oh, I don't know. How about until I take a drink? Not when I pick my drink up, but when I actually drink."

"That's...I...yes, ok, I can agree to that." Now the idea was in his head, he was already starting to think about her naked and wrapped around him.

"Once we walk through that door, it will officially begin."

"Oh god." The door was in sight.

"Do you want to tap out already?"

"No, nope, we are going to do this." *And I'm probably going to be embarrassed by my mother and brother until I can't look you in the eye.* He pulled himself together, took a steadying breath, and prepared to enter the loft.

"Ready?"

"Wait." Sebastian took half a step back.

"What?"

"May I pash you first?"

"Pash?"

"Yeah, it means to kiss. Like a passionate kiss."

"Oh. So pash is short for passionate then?"

"Um." He tilted his head, thinking. "I guess. I never thought about it, but...nah yeah. Never looked up where the word came from, just know I enjoy pashin' on you. Some of my friends used to tease me about it."

"Why? I think it sounds sweet."

"It's a little bit outdated, but my parents always used it, and I guess it just stuck. They had such a great relationship." He trailed off and shrugged.

"Uh huh." She made him shift around awkwardly before giving him an answer. "Well, I suppose you may 'pash' me, Handsome."

"Thank you, Goddess." He leaned down and took confidence from the kiss. *I can do this. We can do this.* "All right, I'm ready." At his nod, Gwen dug the key out of his pocket and opened the door.

"Hey, look who I met while I was waiting for food!" Sebastian strode in smiling and stepped aside to reveal his Domme as she finished closing the door behind them. "This is Gwen." He beamed proudly, especially when his brother missed the counter trying to set his beer down. She was always a ten in his eyes, but he wasn't blind to the way other people reacted to her presence.

"Oh! How wonderful to finally meet you," their mother gushed. "I'm Debbie, Sebastian's mom. He's been so mysterious. I didn't even know he had a girlfriend until Nate told me. This is my youngest son, Nathaniel." She tugged the other man the rest of the way over.

"Hello, it's nice to finally meet you." He shook her hand and smiled. "Sorry about the, uh, party crashing. Bas isn't normally so 'mysterious', as mum put it, so I thought I needed to spring it on him if we were ever going to make it happen."

"Well, it's lovely to meet both of you." Gwen noticed Nate stood a smidge taller than his older brother but was narrower in build with clean-cut dark hair and a smooth face. His voice didn't have the same deep undertones as Sebastian's.

"My, you're so pretty! Sebastian?" She spotted him moving toward the bathroom after putting the food on the table, red shirt in hand. "What are you doing, sweetie?"

"Oh, I was planning on changing shirts before Nate showed up. Just going to do it before we sit down to eat."

"Why don't we go ahead and get everything ready?" Gwen fished silverware and plates out to set the table. Outside the rain began to come down in a steady drizzle and thunder rumbled in the distance. She thought about Sebastian stripping down as quickly as possible and tried not to smile. The open concept of Sebastian's loft was excellent for entertainment, with the only separated area being the bathroom. She glanced across the long space to his bed, pushed under the windows on the far wall, and started planning for later while she straightened each place setting. "Sebastian tells me you live in Croton-on-Hudson. I hope the traffic wasn't too bad driving into the city."

"Not at all. It's always worth it to come see my boys. So, how long have you two been seeing each other?"

"Mum, is that necessary?" Sebastian emerged from the bathroom, feet shifting awkwardly once or twice as he moved to help Gwen. "You don't normally lead with that one."

"I don't mind. Why don't you grab me one of those vanilla sodas from the fridge and ask your mom what she'd like?" Gwen smiled sweetly and watched his expression change slightly.

"Yes, I'm sorry. What would you like, mum?"

"I'll just have water. You're so handsome in red!"

"Thanks, just trying something new." Sebastian moved quickly, getting two glasses with ice and filling with water for his mom. "Here you are."

"Thank you, sweetie!"

"Mhm." He caught the back of Gwen's chair before she could reach it. "Allow me."

"Thank you."

"Mum," he said, pulling out her chair as well. Thinking about Gwen naked was starting to get uncomfortable, but he stayed focused as he poured her drink and handed it to her. She sipped slowly, eyes watching him humorously over the rim. *I love that devious mind of hers.* "Ready to eat?"

"Where's my drink? I could use another coldie," Nate said, frowning. "I'd like to complain to the manager about poor service."

"Get your own, Nate." Sebastian pulled each package of food towards him and separated everything out. He set his brother's to the side while Nate grabbed another beer, but he carefully served his mother, Gwen, and then himself. Sebastian glanced quickly around the small, square table. "Everyone have what they need?"

"I'm good," his mom said cheerily.

"Yes, I think I have everything I need. This…soda is pretty good."

"Oh! Did Sebastian tell you yet? I brought some vanilla slice with me for dessert! Well, it's more of a chocolate-blackberry slice, but it's the same basic idea."

"That sounds delicious! I can't wait to try some." She looked at Sebastian, who froze in uncertainty. *I forgot to decide if my rule would include anyone else saying the word.* "I don't think I've ever had 'vanilla slice' before." Gwen took a dainty bite of her roasted duck and tried not to laugh. "To answer your question, Mrs.—"

"Oh, please." The older woman waved her hand and smiled, unaware of her oldest son's predicament. "Call me Debbie."

"Debbie." Gwen smiled politely and gave a short nod, but she wanted to squirm under the familiarity. *It's fine. Settle down.* "Sebastian and I have been spending time together for about six months."

"Since January? Wow. He didn't say anything at our Easter dinner. He should have invited you. That would have been fun!"

"We'd just started seeing each other more formally, Mum, I didn't want to rush her." Sebastian's mind picked right back up where it left off and was starting to get more creative than just imagining her without any clothes. *The softness of her skin, the smell of her hair, her tongue dragging acro—* He watched Gwen take a sip of her drink. *I can't wait for later.*

"Sebastian knows I want to take things slowly and make sure there are clear expectations and boundaries. So many people forget these days boundaries are a crucial part of any healthy relationship."

"And safe," he said, inclining his head to her.

"Do you have any music we can put on, Bash?" Nate nudged a dumpling around his plate.

"Uh, no." He gave his brother a subtle look begging him not to mess with the sound system. Sometimes they used music as a part of their sessions, and Gwen was particular about what was on her playlist. If anyone hit play, all pretense of this being a normal relationship would be gone. "How are things going with Nicole?" he asked, trying to change the subject.

"Good, good." Nate relaxed visibly at the mention of his fiancée. "She refuses to pick a date though."

"Has she at least picked a venue?" Sebastian didn't notice the sudden interest on his mother's face.

"Narrowed it down to a few. One of 'em is back home."

"Oh? She's thinking of having the wedding in Australia? Wouldn't that be wonderful?" Debbie beamed at the thought and scooped some more rice onto her plate before either son could reach for it.

"I suppose there isn't much sense in picking a solid date until there's a venue. If she picks a day they don't have open, she'll end up having to change one of her choices." Gwen knew a little about trying to plan a wedding—she'd almost married twice.

"I just hope Nicole is happy with whatever she picks. Everything should fall into place a little more easily after that." Debbie looked slyly from Sebastian to Gwen, trying to read their situation. "My son tells me you don't live too far from here. Do you usually walk?"

"It depends on the weather, but a little extra exercise is good, so I walk as much as possible."

"What do you do for work?"

"I'm an editor at one of the Big Five imprints. I handle mostly developmental edits and sometimes the final proofing stages."

"She does a bit of art, too. A couple of her pieces are going to be in a local gallery starting next month," Sebastian said proudly.

"Oh? What kind of art do you make?" Nate cut in quickly and steered the conversation away from where he was sure his mom wanted run with it.

"I do mostly line art in ink, but sometimes I'll do a bit of watercolor. The pieces that'll be in the gallery are all paintings."

"What's your subject? Anything in particular? I'm usually partial to digital art, but I've seen some pretty amazing things in traditional mediums." Nate truly did have an interest in the arts, and he liked Gwen more knowing that she did, too.

"I do whatever comes to mind—I don't limit myself."

"That's wonderful," Debbie chimed in. "It's good to have hobbies outside of the relationship, it gives you something to talk about when you're together again." She was starting to pick at her food and pay more attention to the conversation. "Any siblings?"

"Um, no. I'm an only child." Gwen was suddenly dehydrated and took a very long drink, not stopping until the first hiccup made her choke. *And I need a break.* "Excuse me for a moment." She rose from her chair, letting out a series of cute hiccups. Sebastian stood but could only watch as she went to hide in the bathroom and Nate chided their mom about "scaring her off." "This is ok. Nothing to worry about." Gwen splashed water on her face and reminded herself she was with her Knight. *There's nothing to be afraid of.*

"Are you all right?" Sebastian's concerned voice floated through the door.

"Yes, I just need a minute." *See? It's fine.*

"If it helps, Nate got a call and has to head off. He's convinced mum to go with him." He heard her sigh but couldn't tell if it was relief or frustration. "Gwen?"

"I'm all right." She opened the door, anxiety, and hiccups under control again. "Shall we?" Gwen took the arm he offered and walked back to the table where his family was preparing to leave.

"Sorry to cut this short, but you know how it is, Bash." Nate gave his brother a hug and whispered something. "Gwen, great to meet you finally, hope to see more of you," he said, shaking her hand.

"Yes, you *must* talk Sebastian into bringing you to our next get-together. We'll be having a little something in August at my place and I'd love to show you the house. I think you'd like it out there."

"I'll see what I can do about him. It was very nice to meet you." Gwen tried not to flinch when Debbie hugged her. Once they finally left, she sank into her chair at the table and tried to relax. She closed her eyes when Sebastian started rubbing her shoulders. *What can I say? He already knows it isn't just the anxiety. Did I ruin the night? Did I make a bad impression?*

"Shall we finish dinner?" He knelt and put his head in her lap when she indicated no. Sometimes the little touches helped her reestablish control of herself. Sebastian rubbed his cheek against her thigh as she ran her fingers absently through his hair.

"That wasn't too bad," she finally said.

"No, it wasn't. I think it went great given we were caught off-guard."

"I'm sorry we didn't make it to dessert. It sounds delicious."

"We can eat it later. It'll keep in the fridge."

"I don't want us to change because of others' expectations."

"We won't. Every choice we make is our own. And we don't have to go to any family gatherings if we don't want to."

"And what do we say to get out of that? What excuse do we give for not going after your mom invited me?"

"I will handle my mum. You don't need to worry about her." Sebastian considered his next words carefully. "Despite how it came about, I am glad they met you. You're an important part of my life. True, I want to keep you all to myself, but I'm also very proud to have such an amazing woman. There's no one else I want to be my Goddess." He chanced a look to see if he could read her features. *She's calmer. Good.* "And there's no need for this to cramp our night. I'd still love to know what you planned for us."

"Do you now?" she asked with a small laugh. "Well, you did follow the rules."

"Every single one." He scooped Gwen up, careful not to put too much pressure on her sensitive ribs, and carried her to the winged back chair. "I'll put everything away." After he set her down, Sebastian turned the lights low and started clearing the table.

Gwen watched him clean up from the comfort of her chair. *Dinner didn't go terribly*, she admitted. It could have even been labeled a partial success if she were actually his girlfriend and didn't have anxiety every time she met a guy's family. Too many tricks, too many lies, too many times her giving nature had been mistaken for submissiveness and abused. Sebastian was something completely new and just as uneasy about involving family. *The family visit wasn't intentional. He cares too much and is too considerate to do that.* She closed her eyes, listening to him put the last of the dishes away and take out the trash. The loft fell silent, and she relaxed into the chair.

"Goddess?"

"Hm?"

"You fell asleep."

"Did I? Sorry, it's been a long week and sitting here is so comfortable. I don't think I want to get up." She stretched and opened her eyes to find him sitting at her feet with a coy smile across his face.

"Is there anything I can do for you?" Sebastian removed her shoes and started rubbing her feet. "Anything at all?" He ran his hands up her leg, pushing her skirt up as he went, and kissed her knee. The garter snaps came undone easily and he slid her sheer stockings off. "Please?"

"Now that you mention it, you can keep going in that direction. Without your hands to help." Gwen gently nudged him back with her toes and went to get her bag.

"Mm." Sebastian snuck another kiss as she walked by. "Oh, Goddess, how divine you are."

"Where are your eyes?"

"Admiring the best thing that's ever happened to me."

"And that is?" She returned and spread her kit out on the coffee table. "Hm. Just black tonight, I think," she muttered, pulling out a few coils of rope.

"You, of course."

"Am I?" She kept her tone teasing, but the idea made her happy.

"Yes, and I'm ready to be of service. Please, do with me as you will."

"Think you can handle some hands-free dessert?"

"Absolutely." He licked his lips and started slipping off the red shirt when a knock sounded at the door. "I swear I'm going to put up a 'do not disturb' sign." He stumbled his way to answer the door. "Nate?"

"Hey, Bash." Nate stood outside and waved at Gwen through the space in the door. "Don't need to come in, but since the coast is momentarily clear, I thought I'd give you two what was supposed to be my 'happy you're dating my brother' gift. Enjoy!" Nate tossed a small, poorly wrapped box at his brother's head and disappeared cackling.

"Just when I though he couldn't be any weirder." Sebastian closed the door and turned the oblong box around while he shook his head at the crooked green paper taped around it. "I'm guessing this is probably more for you."

"Why don't you open it? And you may return to calling me by my proper title."

"Yes, my Goddess." He settled back on the floor while she continued preparing and opened the gift. "Ah. Hm. His idea of a joke?" Sebastian held up a traditional feather duster, complete with a long wooden handle in black. "I don't recall this being on my list."

"Maybe not, but I'm sure I can find a use for it." Gwen pursed her lips and took the new toy from Sebastian. "So many possibilities. Now, take off your clothes." She hobbled his elbows before moving to his wrists. They'd been working on his flexibility, and Sebastian was able to keep his arms in previously less-comfortable positions for longer periods of time. Not once in their experimenting had he felt the need to use his safe word. Gwen shifted him closer to the edge of her chair and made him kneel while she bound his calves and connected the knot to his wrists. The mat placed at the foot of her throne was as much for the benefit of his knees as that of her tired feet. Normally, she blindfolded him before she undressed, but tonight she had other plans. Gwen watched Sebastian bite his lip while she unzipped her skirt and let it fall to the floor. Her black bodice was the next piece to go followed by her blouse. The black lace of her bra and panties made her skin glow in the dim loft. "You ate quite a lot for dinner. Do you have room for dessert?"

"Uh huh." Sebastian swallowed, unsure if he was drooling or if his mouth was dry. "If my Goddess is willing to feed me, I'm still very hungry." With nothing on, he couldn't downplay how hard her teasing made him. He loved being so exposed for her.

"Good." Gwen finished unhooking her bra and slid her panties off before sitting back in her chair. She reached over him, stretching to pick up the blindfold she intentionally left on the table, and smiled when Sebastian didn't react to her breasts pressing against him. The final restraint hung innocently from her finger. "I wonder if I should use this tonight. I'm not sure you want it."

"Please, Goddess, please blindfold me." Sebastian shivered as his sight was cut off and Gwen ran her fingers through his hair. He felt her guide his head back toward her knees.

"You may pick up where you left off." She watched Sebastian kiss his way along the inside of her thigh and decided to toy with him just a little more. Hand still on his head, she halted his progress. "Where are your manners, my Knight?"

"Please, Goddess, may I continue? I'm very hungry tonight."

"You may."

"Thank you, Goddess, for this meal." When she allowed him to, Sebastian buried his face between her legs. Tongue searching, he loved that she was already wet. He licked and nuzzled until she cried out in pleasure. He tasted her orgasm and continued until she came again.

"Oh, you are amazing with your mouth, but I think I'm ready for some dessert of my own." Gwen nudged him back and leaned forward to undo the hitch keeping his hands and feet together. She did a quick check, making sure the remaining knots weren't too tight before laying him on the floor. They kept a pillow nearby for these nights, and she pulled it under his head. "Remember: you must wait until I give you permission."

"Yes, my Goddess." Sebastian tensed as his Domme kissed her way down his chest and abdomen while she stroked him. Her tongue teased, flicking over his tip, and running along his erection before she finally took him into her mouth. He moaned and tried not to come yet. Gwen stopped and started, working him to the edge and easing him back again. It was sweet torture he knew would end when she chose, and she only allowed him to find release in one place. She made Sebastian sit up when she straddled him, so he wasn't laying on his arms anymore. He was glad she was always considerate, no matter how eager she was to have him. When he was finally inside her, he put his face in the crook of her neck and moaned again. "Goddess, may I come?"

"Not yet." Knowing how sensitive he could be, Gwen started slow and deep, enough to drive herself over the edge without pushing him too far. She took her time building up the pressure again, and Sebastian shook with the effort of restraining himself the second time she came.

"Please," he begged. "Please."

"Come for me." She quickened her pace and tightened around him as she orgasmed again. A moment later he joined her with a muffled cry that sounded vaguely like her name. Gwen waited until her heart rate was under control and took a steadying breath. "Are you all right?"

"Yes, Goddess," he said, still panting. "Thank you." Sebastian stretched and laid back while she unbound him. The blindfold was always the last to come off, and this time he kept his eyes closed a little longer than usual. He sensed her sitting next to him, carefully putting everything away and rechecking his hands and feet. He caught her hand as it caressed his cheek, leaving a light kiss on the palm before giving her a tired smile. "I'm ok. It was definitely a long week, but well worth the wait."

"Do you want to talk about it?" Over the months, they'd become accustomed to venting to each other and sharing their frustrations with mundane life once the playing was finished. She was happy their relationship wasn't strictly sex and bondage. Their connection was real.

"Just boring business stuff I thought would never end, but here you are. My respite, my sanctuary, my Goddess. May I bask in your divinity a while longer?"

"You want to bask in bed or here on the floor?" she asked with an amused expression.

"How about the couch? I bought that movie you've been wanting to see, and there's ice cream in the freezer if you want it. Or we could have some chocolate slice." Sebastian kissed the hand he still held again and slowly opened his eyes to look at her. Long, dark hair framed her petite face and cognac eyes searched his blue ones. *My elegant Goddess*, he thought happily. Her features held a question he couldn't make out. "Are you ok? I know it's late—we can just go to bed if you're tired. Whatever you want to do."

"What do you want?"

"Whatever you desire, my Goddess," he said, a little confused by the question.

"We're not playing right now, Sebastian. Tell me what you want."

"You. Always." *Oh. Everything from tonight, meeting my family, being welcomed by them, must be a lot to take in.* He wanted to ask her something important, but the question had been stuck in that little spot between his chest and throat where important things often stopped, refusing to be spoken. Sebastian was afraid of asking, afraid it might damage the dynamic they already enjoyed, and worried how it might seem coming on the coattails of dinner. *What'll I do if she says no? Or what if she says yes, and then things don't work out?* "I want you, Gwen, as my Domme and as my...my girlfriend," he said, finally forcing the truth out of himself. Sebastian held his breath.

"I see." After a moment that stretched a little longer than intended, Gwen leaned down to rub her nose against his. "You need to go brush your teeth before you kiss your girlfriend."

"Um, not to be sassy, but you need to brush yours, too."

"Oh, well, in that case." She jumped up. "Me first!"

"Naturally." Sebastian admired the view as she sashayed towards the bathroom, confidence restored. He followed her and snagged his own toothbrush from the counter. "May I join you?"

"Mhm." Gwen finished with her teeth and pulled his free arm around her waist. "You want to get a shower?"

"Not yet." He rinsed his mouth and tugged her back into the living room. "Cuddle with me, Love."

"Wait. I have something for you." She grabbed her purse from the coffee table and flopped onto the couch, patting the cushion next to her. "Come."

"Ok. What's this?" The package she handed him was covered in bright red paper and only an inch or so thick. Sebastian opened it slowly, treasuring the care she'd taken in wrapping the gift and nestled in layers of cream-colored tissue paper was a deep green leather journal. "This is...."

"I know it's a little early, but since you'll be in Australia for your actual birthday, I wanted to give you this now."

"It's similar to yours." He ran his hand over the cover and breathed in the scent of leather and parchment.

"That's the idea. You can write about anything in there, but my hope is for you to use it to write down your thoughts after sessions. What you did or didn't like, or if you think of something you might want to do differently. And you can record any questions, interests, or new things you might want to try."

"Can I talk about you in here?"

"Of course."

"Good. Sometimes I get little ideas—bits and pieces of poetry stuff—I want to share with you, but I forget a lot of it. It's not as good as yours though."

"I love your poetry." Gwen smoothed his hair and kissed his scruffy cheek.

"Maybe this'll help me sort my thoughts when I'm having trouble voicing something. Will you read it?"

"My hope is for us to reach a level of trust where you're comfortable with me reading it, but I won't until you're ready. Maybe through this we can continue making our relationship stronger—especially now. I think it'll help us work through issues we come across."

"That's a wonderful idea."

"Do you like it?" Gwen couldn't read his features well, but he seemed lost in thought.

"I love it. This is probably the most thoughtful gift I've gotten in a long time. Thank you, Goddess." Sebastian set it on the table and hugged up to Gwen. "I wish you were coming with me."

"This trip is for you to spend time with your family. I'll still be here when you get back."

"I know. Maybe another time we could take a trip together—just the two of us."

"Yeah, I'd like that. Now, why don't you carry me to bed."

"As you desire, but I have something for you, too." Sebastian picked Gwen up and took her to bed. "And here. It. Is." From the nightstand he grabbed a palm-sized red dragon with a key hanging from one end. "You can come here any time you want."

"Is that a Welsh dragon?"

"Mhm."

"You're adorable." Gwen accepted the keychain with a kiss.

"Only for you."

5

Gumdrop Buttons

October 31st

"I look ridiculous."

"You look adorable." Gwen adjusted Sebastian's suspenders and smiled. For his Halloween costume, she dressed him in brown slacks and a brown, button-down shirt. It didn't help the man's disposition that both items were decorated with white trim meant to mimic icing and the buttons were little gumdrops. He was the Gingerbread Man, and she was the Baker, dressed in a short, white skirt and a white baker's frock. "Now, when someone asks what you are—"

"I'm a cookie." Sebastian was in the middle of a full man-pout, but his Domme's long legs in a short, tight skirt were distracting as she moved around him to make sure he was ready. He frowned when she came back around with something else in her hands. "A hat? With a *candy cane* sticking out?"

"Do as you're told." Gwen smoothed his hair and positioned the hat lopsided.

"Am I being punished for something?"

"No, I just want everyone to know that I caught you." Her smile widened and she produced a length of soft, creamy white rope.

"Oh. *Oh,*" he said, finally understanding the joke while she bound his wrists and kissed him lightly. "That's pretty clever."

"I know." Gwen winked and double-checked the knots before making sure her own costume was in order. She wove her dark hair into a pair of long braids that draped over each shoulder and put a small baker's hat on. "Move your hands around for me."

"Move around how?"

"Just however you can. I want to make sure you can grab things, like a glass or your phone." She watched him flap his fingers around and stick his tongue out.

"I'm fine. These are pretty loose, actually."

"Don't pout. It's for your safety. Now, let's go." Gwen grabbed the rope and tugged him out the door after her. They breathed in the crisp air as they walked to the club, Sebastian trailing a step behind her. "Are you enjoying the view?"

"Mhm." It was almost enough to distract him from his costume. He stumbled forward and caught himself when Gwen stopped. "What's wrong?" A man with short, black hair in roughed up jeans and a fake cowboy hat glared at them from the other side of the street they were preparing to cross. Sebastian noticed Gwen close off, all the playfulness gone from her attitude. He swore the temperature fell a few degrees around them. The traffic light changed. She didn't hesitate. He followed her as she strode into the crosswalk, radiating careless confidence to the world but clearly upset to him. Dutifully, he kept his eyes forward and pretended to ignore the man who eyed them angrily as he stomped by. "Who was that?"

"My ex," she said when they were safely across and half a block away. Gwen clutched her side instinctively.

"I see." He chewed on that information for a moment. "That's the one who—"

"Broke my ribs, yes." She continued toward their destination. "He's not worth our time."

"Of course." *I won't let him hurt you.* Sebastian kept the words to himself, knowing the most help he could be right now meant fulfilling his role and supporting Gwen emotionally, so she felt safe. Still, he stayed aware of their surroundings as they continued toward the Collared Heart and hoped that was the last they'd seen of her ex. The sun had yet to dip below the horizon and already the general line to get in the club spread past the little clock shop four doors down. Being a partial owner and founding member had a lot of perks, including skipping the line. He followed Gwen through the door to check in with Renee. "Goddess?"

"We'll just mingle for a bit and get a read on things. We don't have to stay long."

"After all the effort you put into our costumes? We can stay as long as you want." Sebastian snuck a kiss on her cheek and set his chin on her shoulder. "Anything in particular you're up for?"

"No, I just want to relax." Gwen reached back to squeeze one of his hands, letting him know she was all right.

"As it pleases you." They made their way into the club and wove through the bodies thronging around the main bar but didn't get very far before a familiar voice got their attention.

"Oh, Gwen, I'm so glad you're here." Fabian rushed over to greet them. His normally green hair was pink and crowned with a pair of yellow pom-pom antennae, and he flitted around like the butterfly he was dressed as. "Hi, Bashie!"

"Hi, Fabian." Sebastian waved awkwardly.

"What are you supposed to be?"

"A Cookie Man."

"Mhm, you sure are." Fabian giggled behind his hand and turned his attention back to Gwen. "And you must be the 'baker' in this little duo. Love it, babe!"

"Thanks, Fab." They exchanged cheek kisses. "What's going on?"

"We have a little emergency, and I was hoping you could help us out." When Gwen nodded encouragingly, he made a pained face that said he knew she probably wasn't going to be thrilled with the request. "Elira's sick and she was supposed to perform tonight. Everyone's expecting a rope show and you're the only other one who's worked with the triplets. *Please*," he said, drawing out the word in a begging tone.

"I can't." Gwen shook her head, braids bouncing slightly against her shoulders. "Bash and I are exclusive. I won't work with anyone else."

"Well," Sebastian said, noticing the disappointment on Fabian's face. "I've never gotten to see you in action. Maybe just this once?" He shrugged.

"A reasonable man! I'm impressed by him again, Gwen."

"Are you sure?" She turned to Sebastian, arms folded, and looked into his blue eyes seriously. "You can't take it back once I'm up there, and you may not like it."

"I'm pretty sure I'm going to enjoy watching you work. Normally, I don't get the opportunity," he said, trying to deflect with humor.

"Not complaining at getting approval from the important party here, but I have to reinforce what Gwen's saying, Bash." Frowns didn't look right on Fabian. "Say your safe word all you want, scream it even, but once she's on stage, she's committed. Are you sure you're ready to see your Domme working with someone else?"

"I'll be fine." Sebastian leaned in to whisper in her ear. "I promise I won't pitch a fit or make a scene, Goddess. I want to see more of what you can do."

"All right, you heard the man, Fab. When do I need to be ready?"

"Yes! I'll tell the triplets right away. You go on in twenty, dove." Fabian rushed off with an excited bounce in his step.

"I guess that means I should head back now and work things out with the girls. Need to make sure we're all on the same page." Gwen tugged on the end of the rope she was holding, forcing Sebastian to inch closer so she could kiss him. "Don't forget whose 'Cookie Man' you are while I'm away."

"Never." He was a little worried, but a quick scan of the club revealed no lurking ex had followed them. After she left, Sebastian found a spot along the edge of the upper level that let him see across the crowd of people below. Being in the club was different now that he was with Gwen. Some of the other fetishes still made him uncomfortable, but he respected that their kinks weren't his, and that didn't make them any less valid. He leaned against railing and waited for the show to begin.

Light flared up across the room from him and washed the stage in watery blues and greens. The curtain drew back, revealing three figures in pale green leotards crouched on the floor ignoring the audience that had fallen silent. Sebastian watched his Domme, still dressed in her short white skirt, step on stage with a mic in hand. She'd left her frock and hat backstage and wore a simple, long-sleeved V-neck. Gwen's dominance showed in the way she carried herself and the little subtle, but powerful, touches. Even from across the room, her presence wrapped around him. Sebastian licked his lips.

"Good evening, everyone, and a very Merry Mischief Night to you all! I hope everyone is enjoying some safe, sane, and consensual shenanigans tonight." Gwen winked, and the audience laughed. "Not all of you know who I am, especially since it's been a while since I've done any shows, and thus introductions are in order. You may address me as Lady Gwen, a dear friend of the Collared Heart's owner and a former student of Mistress Elira and her epic rope skills. Unfortunately, she's unwell, so you're stuck with me." A few people shouted excitedly and clapped. "Sometimes these performances are arranged to be educational, but tonight's is about reveling in the beauty of the human body and all the delicious ways we can bind it, mold it, and even suspend it. I'll be working with the three lovely ladies on stage with me, and you're sure to be delighted by what we have planned." She traded the mic for a small bundle with someone off-stage and returned to the center. A hush fell over the audience.

Sebastian held his breath.

The triplets waited expectantly but never looked at Gwen. Unlike her approach with him, she produced three green sashes and blindfolded them first. Her face held no passion or excitement, just cool, calm focus. This show was business for her, a simple favor for a friend. *She's worked with them before,* he reminded himself. Sebastian admired how she looked on stage—sexy and confident, she was in the spotlight without making herself the primary focus. Gwen was all he could see until she began to work her rope magic on the first of the redheads. The girl's expression changed from stoic to eager, her anticipation building as Gwen built her knots. Something unfamiliar in their time together stirred in Sebastian's stomach: jealousy.

"Gwen's a wonderful artist." Fabian appeared at his elbow, glittery makeup glinting in the low light.

"Yeah. She's amazing."

"The triplets belong to the one who taught her how to tie a knot right. She used to perform from time to time, mostly with Elira, and taught some classes. Life got in the way. You know how it is," he said as he eyed the 'Cookie Man.' "And I can see why she's not started up again despite being more active with the lifestyle."

"What do you mean?"

"Gwen has an unusual style that's caused issues for her in the past, typically in the form of aggressively dominant boyfriends assuming she's submissive. 'Gentle Domming.' People usually assume all Dommes enjoy inflicting pain and degrading their subs because that's the image most commonly presented." Fab pursed his lips. "Your lady isn't a sadist, and you are definitely not a masochist. A rope bunny, yes. Well," he snickered, "maybe not a 'bunny.' A rope 'puppy' perhaps, and you're a service sub. She loves to be serviced, *needs* to be, whether it's having you bound and kneeling at her feet or doing...other activities."

"The night we met she tried explaining her style to me, but I didn't get it until we started playing together. I enjoy what we have. It's rewarding. Fulfilling."

"Good. As I said, I can see why she's stopped, and I'm glad she's found someone steady. Having that sort of bond is important."

"What do you mean she stopped? How long has it been since the last time she did a show?"

"Why did you agree to let her go up there?" Fabian asked, deflecting the question. "You could have said no."

"I wanted to see her work."

"A look from the outside." The other man nodded thoughtfully. "I get that. But now you regret it. I can see it on your face."

"Maybe," Sebastian said with a deep frown. "Maybe I just understand better now." Gwen moved on to the next girl.

"Finding a new limit. That's good. Just be sure you tell her in a calm, rational way later. Gwen doesn't take well to being bossed around or bullied."

"I know. And I won't make a fuss or ruin the show."

"Wasn't worried about that."

"Then what are you worried about?"

"That you might be so jealous and hurt you walk out on her. She left those knots loose enough you could undo them if you needed to."

"Why would I walk out?" Sebastian finally stopped starting at the stage to look at Fabian, very confused. "I'm not upset with *her.* I'm upset with myself and jealous of the girls. That's on me."

"Once more you impress me, Bashie. That's a very mature response."

"I'm not a child, Fab. I can admit my faults and deal." He turned his attention back to Gwen, who was in the process of checking on the first two girls. When she started binding the final triplet, Sebastian told himself to relax.

"Well, I think you're about to be *very* impressed with your Domme. The last time they did this configuration was over a year ago, so only a few people here tonight have seen it before."

"Configuration?"

"Just watch." Fabian examined Sebastian's face as Gwen first raised a large metal circle wrapped with green into the air, followed by the three girls, each bound and suspended to form an "s" at different angles. Once everything was in place, they formed a perfect Celtic triskele pattern in the air. The audience applauded and Fabian laughed at Sebastian's shocked face. "Told you."

"What just happened?"

"Like I said, she's a wonderful artist. Gwen does patterns and fun things with suspension shows, although she's never done anything too outrageous." Fabian patted Sebastian's shoulder. "But you don't strike me as the suspension type."

"No, but that was...amazing. I thought she was just, like, you know."

"Tying them up? Depends on the show, but Elira usually goes a bit more elaborate, so Gwen knew the audience had high expectations. And I knew she wouldn't disappoint." The girls only stayed airborne for a short while—Gwen always erred on the side of caution, and another act was set to follow hers, so she had to keep on schedule. Ever alert, Fabian watched her take a bow and start unwrapping the first part of her performance. "Do you want to go backstage after?" He shot Sebastian a sly little grin.

"What? Oh, I don't know. She's pretty strict about her aftercare. I don't want to interrupt." Sebastian wasn't sure he could behave himself if he went back.

"The triplets are wallow-ers, so she's pretty much just going to tuck them in together and come back out."

"I can wait," he said a little too quickly.

"Are you afraid you're going to break your promise? You are!" Fabian giggled. "You're so cute, Bashie." The butterfly kissed his cheek and darted off toward the door leading into the employees-only area, leaving Sebastian to watch the rest of Gwen's show alone.

Sebastian refused to let his moment of jealousy dampen the night. When Gwen emerged, Sebastian put on a smile and kissed her while he told her how amazing she was. The rest of the party went smoothly, and as the clock turned over to midnight, they said their goodbyes and headed home. They stayed silent during the walk back to his place. He reminded himself to be alert, in case the man from earlier reappeared, and he scrutinized everyone they passed. Sebastian's building was quiet except for one party on the first floor, and by the time they reached his apartment, Gwen was noticeably ready to take her shoes off.

"Did you have a good time?" she asked as he locked the door. She sat on the couch and waited for him to come to her.

"Yes, I'm glad we went." Sebastian brushed by the coffee table on his way to her, wrists still lightly bound. He didn't present the knots to her. Instead, he slipped her shoes off and started rubbing her feet. "You were amazing."

"Thank you. I was so nervous though. It's been forever since the last time I got on stage." Gwen stretched and yawned. "Why don't we get changed? I don't know if I'm ready for bed, but I definitely want to get comfortable." She stood and Sebastian put his hands on her hips as best he could and pressed his face to her stomach. Startled by the movement, she wobbled and almost fell back onto the couch.

"I'm sorry," he said, trying to hide his face. "You were so great up there."

"What's wrong?"

"It's just...I know I said it was ok, I encouraged you to go, but...." He thought about the triplets' excitement, how happy they looked. "I didn't think it would bother me."

"Bash?" Gwen sat down and lifted his chin; he looked about to cry. She kissed his forehead and took his hat off. "Talk to me."

"I'm not mad or upset with you. I'm mad at myself." He bit his lip and tried to push back his frustration. "Everything was fine until I saw...."

"Until you realized they were enjoying the attention usually reserved for you?"

"Sort of. Yeah. I just got jealous. I wanted it to be me, and only me, but I couldn't—wouldn't—interrupt you. I loved watching you work. I just wanted it to be me." Sebastian looked up at her mournfully.

"It's ok. You're allowed to be jealous." She smoothed his ruffled hair and started tugging the knots loose.

"Do you have to?" He wanted to drift in that sense of belonging to her a while more.

"Yes, it's already been longer than I prefer. We can find something else to do, my Cookie Man, but I still want to get changed."

"All right." He let her finish unbinding him and followed when she pulled him towards the bathroom. Sebastian watched Gwen take off her hat and frock, tossing them into the hamper, before stripping off the shirt underneath and her skirt. He switched on the water for the shower and jumped a little at her hand coming around him to undo the buttons on his shirt. "Goddess?"

"Yes?"

"May I wash you?"

"Why I thought you'd never ask," she said teasingly. Gwen finished with his shirt and slid her hand down to massage him through the gingerbread pants she'd made him wear. "Do you want me?" She grinned at the noise he made when her hand went under the waistband, caressing his skin.

"I always want you." Sebastian freed himself of the shirt and his pants before pulling Gwen into the shower, still in her bra and panties. He propped her against the slate-colored tile so he could kiss along her neck and collarbone, and then moved to tease her breasts through the thin fabric covering them. Tonight, she'd worn something simple so it wouldn't show under her shirt; it still made him hard to see her nipples as the iridescent white satin soaked through with hot water. He unbraided her hair so it could twist in wet ringlets around her body while he knelt and continued trailing kisses down her stomach. Sebastian's fingers made their way down her panties to dip into her. He groaned. "I want you, Goddess."

"That's not washing," she said with a gasp when he tugged her panties off and draped one leg over his shoulder. Gwen grabbed the bar he'd installed for whenever they took their activities into the shower. His tongue and fingers continued exploring while the water cascaded over them. Sebastian didn't stop until she moaned, and he could taste her orgasm.

"*Now*, I will wash you." He smirked and grabbed her shampoo. They'd created many rituals for him to express his reverence and washing her was one of his favorites. Sebastian massaged her scalp, taking care not to tangle her hair much more than it already was.

Next, he lathered her body in wisteria and jasmine scented soap. His hands cleaned every inch of her.

"Your turn." Gwen took pleasure in occasionally washing him, but tonight she watched as he scrubbed himself clean. She noticed he didn't take as much time as he did with her, so she reached a hand out. "Slow down."

"As it pleases you." Sebastian was still a little embarrassed when he felt her eyes on him. It was one thing not to be able to hide his arousal, it was another for her to watch as he stroked himself. Gwen stepped closer, grazing his tip with her body as she brushed her lips against his. Her tongue explored his mouth, and he quickened his pace.

"Take me to bed." The water turned off and although they were still soaked, Gwen didn't let him stop to towel off as they rushed into the other room. "Let's see if you can keep your hands to yourself without being tied up."

"Yes, my Goddess." He barely got the words out before she was on top of him, kissing him fervently and fondling him. Sebastian almost grabbed her hips but stopped just shy of touching her. He put his hands above his head and tried to focus on finding his subspace while Gwen nibbled at his ear and pressed her body against him. When she slid onto his erection, he bit his lip and groaned. He forgot about her ex, the party, the show, and his jealousy while she rode him. She came, and he held back. She pushed him to the edge until he was gasping and shaking with the effort, and still he held back. Sebastian would only allow himself to let go when she gave permission.

"Say it for me."

"Ymroddhi. I surrender." His body was tense with need and anticipation, but saying their word relaxed his mind. This was where he was supposed to be, and all of him belonged to her.

"Come for me, my Knight." Gwen enjoyed the ecstasy on Sebastian's face that came with his release. They were still slick from the shower, and now with sweat, but she laid on his chest and listened to his heart. His breathing slowed, and he wrapped his arms around her. "You know you're the only one I want, right?"

"Yeah," he said with a nod. "I'm sorry. I wasn't doubting you, and I wouldn't give this up for anything."

"True blue?" she asked, trying to use one of his colloquialisms.

"True blue." Sebastian chuckled, not caring to correct her.

"That was wrong, wasn't it?"

"Yup, but it was cute," he said kissing the top of her head. "If you enjoy doing shows, I don't want you to stop. We can figure something out."

"We agreed to mutual exclusivity. I only worked with the triplets as a favor and because you said it was ok. Beyond those circumstances, I work with you and only you."

"Can I ask…why do you love rope so much? What made you take an interest in it?"

"Lots of things. At first, I just loved the aesthetic and the complexity, so I looked into some local events and classes to learn more, and that's how I met Elira. We got to talking about the class she'd helped run, and she invited me to her next event. Fab was excited when I told him about her. One thing led to another, and we asked if she'd be interested in doing some shows at the Collared Heart since it was still getting off the ground, and there weren't too many people performing yet. She became my mentor."

"And the two of you did some performances together?"

"Mhm. It was a lot of fun."

"Was there much to learn? Beyond the different ties, of course."

"Definitely. You can't just dive into it. There are the basic ties which are your building blocks for more complex things, but she also taught me about pressure points, nerves, how ties can be used to achieve different results, and what questions I needed to ask *before* rope even comes out of the bag."

"Like when you asked me if I had any health issues you should know about?"

"Exactly. Old injuries and poor circulation can impact a person's capabilities and response. So, for instance, Fabian broke his shoulder a long time ago, and despite physical therapy and remaining active, he can't do certain positions."

"Right, you two played together."

"Yeah, it's been a long time though. When John was still alive, the three of us would get together, and once it was just the two of us, we used it to heal and work through our shared grief. It helped me find and embrace my 'gentle' Domme side. Fabian's such a wholesome little cinnamon roll, and I wanted to protect him." Gwen propped herself up and ran her fingers over Sebastian's chest. "The more I learned about rope and practiced, the more I fell in love with it. There's a deeper level of intimacy and trust involved that I just don't get from anything else. Binding someone with rope is a conversation between Dominant and submissive." She nipped his lower lip. "A slow, sweet seduction."

"You're doing a good job seducing me without rope right now. I thought you were tired."

"I am."

"Then why are you trying to get me worked up again? Or are you just teasing me?"

"Maybe." She traced the scars along his side. "Will you tell me about these?"

"Hm? Oh, yeah. They're pretty old now." Sebastian rubbed at the scar on his chin self-consciously. The memories weren't pleasant, but he had no reason to keep them from her. "It has to do with why we—my family and I—went home for my birthday this year."

Gwen stopped toying with him and sat up. "What's wrong? Why are you crying?"

"Sorry. I just get a little upset still." He rubbed at his eyes.

"Don't ever apologize for your emotions—they're nothing to be ashamed of."

"But I—"

"Everything you feel is valid and shouldn't be dismissed or hidden. Don't diminish yourself—especially with me. You know I accept all of you."

"I know. You're right. It's...it's hard to let go sometimes. People expect me to be strong all the time and choke it down. But, for you." Sebastian pulled her back down against his chest. "I'll do my best not to hold it in." *Where to begin?* "Before Nate and I took over the company, it was our father's, and he worked all the time. We had a good relationship, but he traveled between offices frequently and put in long hours to provide for us. He was there for every holiday, anniversary, and birthday—until he wasn't."

"What happened?"

"It's...my fault." When Sebastian hesitated, she waited for him to decide he was ready to continue. "For my fifteenth birthday, he promised to take me out to...to.... Hell, I don't even remember now, but I know I'd been looking forward to it for a while. The night before, he called to tell me he wasn't going to make it. I was so angry and disappointed that I yelled and hung up on him. All I could think about was myself and how my birthday was ruined. Selfish. Just…selfish."

"We all get angry with our parents sometimes, especially when they break a promise."

"Maybe, but it was still selfish and uncalled for. Mom got a call early the next morning—four or five, I think. Dad had decided to drive home after his last meeting even though it ran late. He wanted to surprise me, but he must have been exhausted. They said he fell asleep and went off the road. When she told me, I ran out of the kitchen, wasn't paying any attention to where I was going, and slammed into the curio cabinet in the dining room. There was glass and broken dishes everywhere. I'm lucky these scars are all I ended up with. So, ultimately, I ruined my own birthday. He died because I got angry over something stupid, and I never got to apologize or tell my father how much I loved him."

Gwen shifted so she could put her arms around him. "Bash, it's not your fault."

"How is it not? He was coming home. For *me*."

"That doesn't make it your fault, no more than being manipulated and abused by my ex is my fault."

"I don't know. I still feel responsible." Sebastian wanted to be stubborn, to cling to the guilt that had haunted him for much of his life, but Gwen put things into perspective. "Why does that have to make sense?"

"Because it does. You know, when John died, Fabian and I blamed ourselves. It took time, but eventually we realized we couldn't have done anything. I don't expect your outlook to change overnight." She ruffled his hair. "Talk to me. Tell me when you're hurting. I'm here for you."

"Thank you, love. Your support means everything." Eager to change the subject, Sebastian rolled until Gwen was under him and he could shower her with kisses. "Now that we've strayed from my original question."

"Mm?"

"Do you miss doing shows?"

"Sometimes, but I'm good with helping at the club behind the scenes."

"Well, I don't relish the thought of hanging in mid-air, and I'm not an exhibitionist. *But* I saw something on one of the notice boards in the lobby—something about Shibari lessons. What if we did that?"

"We?"

"Yeah, we. I'm not keen on being in front of a large group, but small classes wouldn't be so bad."

"You would do that?"

"Why not? You're attentive and caring—those are good traits to teach others. And we could make it a part of our sessions. You tie me up, and then when we get home you can tell me what a good boy I was. Maybe even reward me?" He massaged her hips and wiggled his eyebrows.

"You're incorrigible, 'Cookie Man.'" Gwen giggled when he wrapped her legs around his waist. "I'm so tired though," she teased. "I might fall asleep."

"Don't worry, Goddess, I'll think of a way to keep you awake."

6

Welcome Home

December 23rd

Sebastian's heart skipped a beat as he stood in front of Gwen's place. A few inches of snow coated the old brick building and the hedges coming up to the bottom of the first-floor windows. Nearly a year had gone by since they met, but this was the first time she'd welcomed him into her private space. His hand trembled as he approached the main door and slid his shiny new key into the downstairs lock. At first, it resisted him, but she'd warned him the front door tended to stick in the winter and with a little wiggling and a bit of oomph, it whined open. Sebastian shook the cold off once he was inside and took the stairs one at a time, listening uncertainly as the wood popped and cracked under his feet. The bright wrapping paper of the package under his arm reminded him of why he was there and the key in his other hand gave him the courage to finish the climb. *Gwen trusts me.* A nickel "3-B" glinted in the yellow light of the third-floor hallway. The door it adorned was plain white and set into the wall on the right side of the building. He swallowed nervously and knocked.

"My Knight." Gwen opened the door and looked him over with a pleased smirk. "Don't you look dashing?"

"Merry Chrissie, Goddess." Sebastian sucked in his breath at the sight of her. He was used to the Gwen who wore tight skirts and sexy lingerie, but he wasn't ready for the comfortable Gwen, the one with her dark hair swept back in a messy bun and wearing an over-sized, red sweater. The black cats with Santa hats were silly but added to the sweet-sexy look. "Wow."

"Merry Christmas. Are you coming?" she asked when he didn't immediately follow her inside.

"Yes." He couldn't quite peel his eyes away from the fact that she wasn't wearing any pants. "They're pink."

"Hm?"

"It smells great. Are you baking?" *I didn't think Gwen wore pink anything, much less panties.*

"Yup. Tradition, and you're going to help me." The first room he walked into was the kitchen, and Gwen moved easily around the tight space as she checked whatever was in the oven.

"What can I do?" He took in the worn wood of the cabinets, the cheery atmosphere, and the warm smell of cinnamon and spice permeating the air. Sebastian felt as if he'd walked into his grandmother's kitchen.

"First, you can put that under the tree." She gestured to the present he carried and waved him into the next room.

"All right." The doorway led into a small, square area stuffed with a couch and her work desk. Built-in shelves overflowing with books carefully organized by genre, then author, covered one wall. The main light came from a bay window letting in the final embers of the day and strings of lights around the room. A Christmas tree took up most of the view outside, and the smell of real fir mingled enticingly with the scents coming from the kitchen. He soaked in the sight of glass and homemade ornaments glittering against white lights wrapped among the branches, the crystal snowflakes and holly hanging along the walls, and the classic Christmas music playing in the background. Cozy. Warm. Home. Gwen's place was completely different from his modern loft. Sebastian was overcome with the urge to take a nap on the couch as he set his gift under the tree. Instead, he went back into the kitchen and hung his coat and scarf on the rack by the door. Her back was to him, so he walked up and slid his hands along her hips to pull her into a hug. He kissed her neck and asked, "What can I help you with, my Goddess?"

"Try this," she said, handing him a gold-brown dumpling that easily fit in his palm.

"Hothothot!" Gooey apple filling flooded his mouth when he bit into the pastry and sparked along his tongue with added flavor. "So good. Mm. What's with the—"

"Extra punch?" Gwen smiled as she watched him devour the rest of it. "I make my own dough, so I put some spices in it to enhance the flavor."

"It's amazing. So, are we skipping tea and going straight for dessert?"

"Tea?" She scrunched her brows in confusion.

"Dinner, I mean. I still call it 'tea' sometimes." He peered around her to see what else he could sample. "I don't think I'll have room for anything for a week with all of this. Not sure how I'm going to tell my mom I won't be eating any of her cooking this year." Sebastian reached for an oatmeal raisin cookie, and she swatted his hand away.

"I've let you spoil your 'tea' enough. Time to eat some real food, and then we'll get back to the baking, some of which is for your mom's." Gwen shooed him around the small island toward a tiny café-style table on the other side of the room. "Sit."

"Yes, my Goddess." He smirked as he obeyed her command and was rewarded with a nice view of her bustling around the kitchen. The table was set for two, with polished silverware and holly-rimmed plates. Sebastian admired the red crystal glasses. "You're really into Chrissie."

"Well, yeah, it's...I just enjoy it." She knelt to look in the oven.

"It's wonderful. Are you sure you don't need help?" he asked, watching her lift a pan into the air.

"I'm sure. You got here just in time." She pulled the neatly folded foil back and exposed a small bird. "The duck is done."

"Not turkey? I thought that was traditional."

"My grandma always made a duck." Gwen set everything out. "It's not much, but since we'll be celebrating with your family on Christmas, I thought we could do something. Just the two of us."

"What about your family? Are we going to see them for the holiday?" Sebastian watched her freeze as she reached for a bottle of wine.

"No." She sat and poured the bubbly rosé. "Let's eat before it gets cold, and then you can help me with a couple more projects tonight."

"Of course." He let her dodge the topic. For now. Gwen asked him about work. He asked how her new contract was coming along. They talked about the big snowstorm due to hit the day after Christmas, and Sebastian suggested spending that time together, as if they hadn't already planned to pass the extended holiday wrapped up in each other. "I've got this," he said when she finished playing with the last bites on her plate. "You cooked, I can clean, and then we can get started with whatever you have planned next." He took their dishes to the sink and discreetly snatched another dumpling from the tray.

"I saw that." Gwen sipped her wine and watched him try to stuff it in his mouth to hide the evidence. "You won't get any treats later if you misbehave."

"Yes, Goddess." Sebastian almost choked on the pastry when he heard the tone of her voice. It made him shiver just a little when she sounded playful and commanding at the same time. He knew if he did as he was told, the night was sure to end with him trussed up under her while she worked them both to a delightfully sweaty mess. *I wonder what her room looks like.*

"You can wash these, too." She started clearing off the various pans and cookie sheets covering the counters and neatly packing the desserts into containers. Some were to take to his mom's, but others were for her own personal stash. Gwen put everything away as he cleaned it, never letting the dishes linger for more than a moment. "Now," she said as he finished, "this is one of our projects for the night." She turned to the island where a couple of pans still lay, their contents covered with cheery, reindeer towels.

"You didn't," he groaned when she yanked the towels back.

"Oh, I did. Freshly made just for you, my Knight. Can you handle that?" She grinned at him wickedly as he stared at the various blank gingerbread cookies and pieces of house waiting to be decorated.

"I can. I will. And I want romantic compensation when we're done."

"If you pass."

"*When* I pass." Sebastian wrapped his arms around her waist to kiss her. "Oh, ye of little faith."

"No, actually, I'm counting on you succeeding. The rest of the night will be much more interesting that way, but I thought it might be a nice bonding activity for us during this festive season." She returned his kiss and picked up the first thing of frosting. "Shall we get to it?"

"Mhm." He built the house while she went to work on the cookies. When she dabbed frosting on his cheek only to lick his ear, Sebastian dabbed some on her nose.

"You better clean that up." Gwen tried not to giggle when he complied, but it was hard when he reached over and brushed her side lightly enough to tickle.

"Accident," he said, feigning innocence with a poorly hid smile.

"Sure, it was." She licked his cheek clean and went back to work. "This is you," she said as she held up the gingerbread man she'd just finished decorating and snickering. Black lines crisscrossed the cookie in a pattern that looked strikingly like a rope harness, while a bit of blue passed over its face for a blindfold.

"Wow. That's...I'm speechless. You turned a holiday pastime into a BDSM display." Sebastian put his head in one hand and laughed before kissing his Goddess. "I love you, Gwen."

"I love you, too, my handsome Ginger-sub." She noticed a silly smile on his face. "What?"

"Nothing. Just enjoying the general...holiday affect."

"What's that mean?" Gwen watched him shrug nonchalantly. "Are you being a brat?"

"No, my Goddess."

"Then tell me what." She set the cookie down and waited.

"You're beautifully dense sometimes," he said with a heavy sigh. Sebastian reached out and yanked her towards him, kissing her deeply. "That's the first time you've told me you love me. Do you mean it?"

"Of course, I mean it." She shoved his shoulder lightly but didn't go anywhere. "Bash...the reason...the reason we won't be visiting with my family for the holidays is because they're gone." Gwen leaned into Sebastian's embrace and took a moment to appreciate his patience while she figured out what to say. "I don't have any family left."

"Do you want to talk about it?"

"I guess."

"You don't have to."

"But you should know." She tightened her arms around him and resolved to give him the truth as plainly as possible. "I never knew my father. My mom was single, and I barely remember her. When I was still very little, she got addicted to...I don't know what she started with, but Child Services took me away and gave custody to my grandparents. She never came to visit or tried to contact me. One day, my grandfather sat me down and said she'd passed away. He didn't tell me she'd died with a dirty needle in her arm in a rundown motel. My grandparents raised me."

Sebastian didn't know what to say. *I think we're done with gingerbread houses for now.* Lifting Gwen, he carried her to the couch where they could cuddle in front of the tree. "So. Christmas was special for you."

"Yes. I was left with them just before Christmas Eve, and I didn't understand what was happening. My grandmother did everything she could to make me feel at home, and it became a tradition. The baking, the cooking, the decorating—all of it. Most of what you see was theirs." Gwen waved her hand in an absent circle.

"Was?" He heard a small sniff.

"About four months before we met, they were in an accident." She buried her face in his chest and pushed the tears back down. "This is my second Christmas without them."

"I wish I'd been able to meet them, but I am glad you want to share your traditions with me. Maybe we can add one of our own?" He felt her nod against his sternum.

"They would have liked you. Grandma always had a keen sense when it came to people. She warned me to get away from...from *him,* but I didn't listen to her. We argued a bit over it, yet when I needed a safe place to get away, she welcomed me home." Gwen lifted her head to look at him, eyes watery. "I miss them."

"You're allowed to, Love." Sebastian wiped away a stray tear. "Just because you're a Domme, doesn't mean you have to be in control a hundred percent of the time."

"I show a lot of weakness with you. Don't you find that frustrating?"

"No, I love it. You trust me not to take advantage of it, you know I won't, and if I know what's bothering you, we can find a way to work through it. Besides, you're also my girlfriend."

"True. Do you want presents now or later?"

"First, tell me about the rest of the situation with your ex." He rubbed her back when she stiffened. "I just want to know. After we saw him at Halloween.... You said he shoved you, broke your ribs, and you ended up in the hospital. What happened?"

"It was more than shoving," Gwen said, closing her eyes and biting her lip. "He was charming at first. *Very* charming. Did everything right, from opening the door to saying all the things I wanted to hear. I should've known something was off, but I guess I didn't want to see it. I wasn't as active in the community at the time, so I didn't have a lot of friends beyond Fabian. Work and side projects kept me busy. He brightened my day just enough and suckered me in.

"The first hit came when we argued about moving in together. 'It was an accident,' he told me. 'I didn't mean it.' I believed him and forgave him. When I took him to meet my grandparents, we went for a normal dinner, no special holidays. I never shared Christmas with him. He...got mad that I wasn't planning to take him with me for the holiday, that I wanted to spend it alone with them. He tried to isolate me from them after that, and when I refused to budge on the subject, he hit me again."

"Gwen." One hand smoothed away her frown. "It's ok."

"The time that I ended up in the hospital, he threw me into a wall because I didn't notice he was wearing a new watch. That was," she paused to count, "four years ago. He went to jail, I retreated from the city for a few months, and then moved into a new place with a new number and everything. That's how I ended up here."

"How long has he been out of jail?"

"About six months. They let me know he got out on good behavior. I didn't think it important to mention at the time, because why would he risk his parole and it was in the past. I still have an order against him, and I doubt he'll bother us."

"But if he does, I will protect you. No one will hurt you." Sebastian held her a moment longer. "Now, let's do pressies."

"All right." Gwen got up to grab a couple of packages from under the tree. "Here. You first." She watched him tear through the paper like a little kid.

"Oh, YES." He admired the silver and black fountain pen. "You even got it engraved. 'My Knight.' I love it, thank you." The other two gifts paired with the pen: a bottle of high-grade ink and a sleek mahogany case to carry the pen in. "These are wonderful. I can't wait to show this off at work." It was a public but subtle claim of ownership, and Sebastian relished the idea of no one but Gwen and maybe his brother knowing what it meant. He rose to retrieve the slim box he'd brought. "Your turn."

"Hm. I wonder what it could be." Gwen took her time unwrapping the gift, treasuring each seam and piece of tape. Her Knight knew how to wrap a present. "Bash." She stared at the contents. Inside she found two plane tickets and a hotel reservation for a trip Australia. "Really?"

"Yes. We can go whenever works for you, but I thought it would be a nice reprieve from the winter weather here. I know we both have the time available."

"Thank you." She leaned in to kiss him. "I guess I should reward you for doing so well earlier."

"Please." Sebastian accepted his Goddess's hand and followed her into the bedroom. Walking into her most private space was surreal. A silver bedspread glinted as she flicked a lamp on, while strands of little white stars lined the walls. The smooth, dark wood of the floor was dotted with silver and blue rugs. "Where did you find furniture this blue?"

"My grandfather repaired and refinished a set for me as a housewarming gift when I moved in here." She trailed a hand over the shiny fabric covering her bed and picked up a length of white and red rope. "So, Cookie Man, tell me what you want."

"Uh." He looked from her bare legs to the candy cane rope in her hands, drawing a blank on where exactly he wanted to start. "Can we do that thing where I pleasure you hands-free?"

"There's no chair in here."

"That's ok, the bed will be just fine." Sebastian closed his eyes when his Domme came over and undid his belt so she could tease him. Underneath the cinnamon and spice, the familiar scent of her perfume wound around him like her fingers in his hair. His jeans slid down his hips and got stuck at his knees while she stroked him. "As much as I love how you look in it, may I take your top off?"

"Yes, and then take your shirt off." Gwen's hand stopped so he could pull the red sweater off her. She watched Sebastian free himself of his shirt and then the rest of his clothes when she gestured to with a nod and a smirk. "Come here." Moving around on the bed to restrain him was awkward, but she laid back to admire her work. His knees were splayed apart for support, and she bit her lip as his abs flexed when he leaned down to nuzzle her bare breasts.

"I couldn't tell you weren't wearing a bra underneath that. How scandalous, Goddess." Sebastian kissed his way down her stomach to grab the top of her pink panties with his teeth and tugged. "May I proceed?"

"You may." She slid them off and put her legs along either side of him. Sebastian's head lowered again, and Gwen ran her fingers through his hair, arching her hips against his tongue. "Tell me you love me again."

"I love you, Goddess," he said, lifting his head slightly to say the words. Before his tongue could go back to work, she stopped him and made him sit back. "Something wrong?"

"Give me more." Wiggling her hips, Gwen moved down the bed so she could go back to stroking his erection. She smiled deviously when he whimpered.

"Goddess?"

"Give me more. Give me everything, my Knight. Say it for me."

"Ymroddhi."

"I love you." Her heart started to race as she guided him. Hard was enveloped by wet and warm as Gwen rubbed against him, tugging his hips toward her in quick jerks that made her orgasm sooner than she meant. Sebastian's expression went from focused pleasure to barely holding on in way that encouraged her to push harder against him. She rolled them over and kept his body pressed against hers. "I want you," she said, voice ragged. Gwen continued thrusting while he throbbed and pushed into her movements until she came again. This time, she changed pace, so his erection stayed deep inside of her. She kissed Sebastian's neck and nibbled his ear, whispering that she loved him. "Now, come for me." With one hand buried in his dark blond hair, Gwen felt his release filling her while he moaned into the crook of her neck.

"Mm." Sebastian's body shook, his mind a pleasant blank as he lingered in his subspace. Being wanted by her, belonging to her, pleasing her—these were his only purpose during their sessions, and all he wanted from life was to remain wrapped up in her.

"I love you, Bash," Gwen said, enjoying the feel of him still inside her while she held him.

"I love you, too. Can we stay here for a while?"

"Of course."

7

Sunbaked

Late January

A salty breeze ruffled the edges of Gwen's book, and she inhaled contentedly. Whitehaven Beach was as stunning as Sebastian promised with pristine white sand and turquoise water lapping at the shoreline. The surprise vacation to the Whitsunday Islands in Queensland, Australia was wonderful. Except for the flying part. The first time the plane jumped in a fit of turbulence mid-flight on the way out of New York, she tried to climb in his lap despite the seatbelt. By the time they boarded their connecting flight in California, she was worn out from the anxiety and spent most of it passed out. They'd arrived safely to their hotel on Hamilton Island with her swearing she'd never watch another horror movie involving planes.

"Ok." Sebastian's tone was as bashful as the first time he told her his safe word. "There's...something I want to try."

"Oh?" Gwen raised her eyebrows and stopped reading—he rarely asked to try anything new. She rolled onto her side to get better look at him and reveled in the sand softly scratching against her skin. "Go on."

"Um." Blushing, he rubbed the back of his neck and glanced down. "So, remember how I said I was all right with being restrained physically and not being able to see, but I wasn't willing to go any further into the whole sensory deprivation…thing?"

"Mhm." His squirming brought a sly smirk to her lips.

"Could we try that thing with the headphones? Maybe?"

"You want me to take away your hearing?"

"Yes?"

"That's not a very confident yes." Gwen sat up and grabbed his chin gently, rubbing her thumb over his lips. "Are you sure?"

"Yeah, I want to try."

"Complete quiet or music?" The turn of events intrigued her. This deeper level of submission required a great deal of trust on his part. *Maybe the vacation is doing some good after all.*

"Music. Definitely music."

"Sure. I don't see why we can't make that happen."

"Great." Sebastian was relieved by her response and went back to enjoying the rush of waves.

"You're still nervous." She watched his posture. "We'll take our time, like always, and we'll start with something quiet." Gwen set her book to the side and moved behind him. "Relax," she said, rubbing his shoulders.

"I'm trying, but I keep thinking about that stupid contract."

"Nate can handle it."

"I know he can. I just…." Sebastian trailed off and sighed. "It's beautiful here, and I'm happy you're with me."

"Good. I was starting to worry you didn't want to be here." Gwen changed tactics and shifted so she was in his lap, running her nails lightly over his bare chest. "Forget work. You're going to pay attention to me."

"Yes, my Goddess." Sebastian admired the black bikini top hugging her breasts and the long gap between it and the top of the blue sarong clinging to her hips. Sometimes he forgot her naval was pierced. He casually slipped one hand under the smooth fabric around her waist, massaging his way up her leg. "It's very quiet here today."

"Mhm." A few people wandered farther down the beach, too busy with their own activities to pay attention to them. Gwen distracted him from thoughts of work with deep kisses.

"Too bad you don't do camping or sailing. We could've stayed here for the night."

"I prefer my modern amenities." She felt his hand move up her leg to play with the edge of her bottoms.

"Goddess, may I?" He started to sneak his fingers under the material.

"No, you may not."

"N-no?" Sebastian stopped, mouth agape.

"No," she said primly. "You'll have to wait. In the meantime, rub some more oil on my back."

"Yes, Goddess." He grimaced when she nestled between his knees and backed herself as close to him as she could, wiggling her hips against his erection. "That's not fair."

"Hm? When did I agree to play fairly?" Gwen retrieved her book while he got to work.

"So, teach me some more Welsh, Love."

"All right. What do you want to learn?"

"How do you say 'finger-lickin' good?'"

"Sebastian."

"Yeah?"

Straight-faced, Gwen turned the page in her book. "'Finger-lickin' good' is an American-English colloquialism that doesn't make much sense when you try to translate it verbatim into another language. It's also a company slogan that, due to advertising, has a specific connotation within American culture that might not translate along with the words. So, whenever I want to say 'finger-lickin' good' in Welsh, or any other language for that matter, I say 'Sebastian.'"

"How am I the brat?"

"Never said I wasn't one."

He hmphed and tickled her sides. "Fine. Teach me something else."

She squirmed and swatted at his hands. "Dych chi'n ddrwg."

"I got the 'you are' part," he chuckled, wrapping his arms around her waist, "but what's the rest?"

"Means 'naughty.'"

"Ohhh. Are you going to punish me then?" Sebastian kissed along her shoulder and nibbled her ear. "Or do I need to be naughtier?"

"This isn't torturous enough for you?"

"Mmm…no." He continued nibbling down her neck. "Please punish me, Goddess."

Gwen wasn't sure what would be the best way to punish him. *I can't physically punish him here—we're in public. Unless I gave him some tasks or something? Or…denial? Something verbal? Something…something…oh. Oh, yes.* "All right, my naughty Knight. I've just the thing for you." She pulled her bag over and rummaged through it. "I didn't think I'd actually need it, but here we are."

"What's in the little black bag?" Sebastian played with the satin bag she passed him, trying to figure out what could be inside. "It's hard…. Metal? Roun—oh." He pursed his lips. "Well, I'll be stuffed."

"With?" She cocked an eyebrow at him.

"N-no, I'm just—it's an expression. I'm just surprised you brought it is all. I, uh," his voice dropped to a whisper, "need to figure out a safe place to go put it on. I'll be right back."

"Mk, marchog drwg."

"Does that mean 'naughty knight'?"

"More or less."

"Yes."

"Hate to see you go, but love watching you leave." Gwen winked at Sebastian when he stuck his tongue out at her over his shoulder. The cage was still a relatively new addition to their collection of toys, but it certainly made things more fun. For her, anyway. There were a lot of pleasurable punishments to choose from, and with his bits under lock and key, she'd have her submissive at her mercy and could deny his orgasm for as long as she wanted. She smirked and muttered, "someone's eager." *I'll be tormenting him for the rest of the afternoon.* And *he wants sensory deprivation? Mm. Yum.* Her mouth watered at the possibilities.

Fifteen minutes later, Sebastian wandered back and placed a small key in her palm. "For you, my Goddess. I submit to your whim."

She tucked the key away and ruffled his hair. "Such a good boy."

He sighed and rubbed his face into her hand. "How may I serve you?"

"Massaaaaaaage." Gwen drew the word out and motioned him behind her.

"Yes, go…orgeous," he corrected when another couple walked by.

"Sans the tickling." She let his hands rove a little bit, but Sebastian behaved himself for the rest of the afternoon. As evening settled in, their guide returned and waved them over, indicating it was time to head back. "Why don't we order room service tonight?"

"You don't want to go out?" He paused in the midst of collecting their things. "I thought we might explore a little."

"Oh, we will, but I thought it might be more relaxing to stay in tonight. We just got here yesterday—there's still plenty of time for you to show me around the islands. Besides, I'm not done punishing you yet." She leaned down, hair spilling over her shoulders, and kissed his nose.

"You just want to tie me up."

"You know you like it."

"True enough." Sebastian finished packing their belongings, and they boarded the small boat that brought them to the beach. They had plenty of time ahead of them to have fun, but the return ride was too short for him. He desperately wanted to cling to each moment. Back in their room, Sebastian leaned against the doorway to the balcony and watched as the setting sun turned the sky bright orange and pink before fading into dusky purple then deep navy and black. A few clouds came in on a strong wind and blocked out the stars. "Sometimes I miss it here."

"Do you want to move back?"

"I don't know," he said honestly. "I have a life in New York that I love, although it wouldn't be impossible to move most of it to Australia. Our office in Sydney will need a new manager here soon since the current gentleman is retiring. There's only one very important part I'm not sure would follow if I did." Sebastian glanced over. "Know what you want?"

"Yes." She walked over, menu in hand, and stood on her tip toes to kiss his neck and nibble his ear. "You know what I like to eat."

"Should I even bother with this then?" he asked with a chuckle as he took the menu from her.

"If you want." Gwen hooked her fingers into the top of his shorts and tugged him back into the room. She sat him on the edge of the bed while she dug around in her suitcase for the bag of toys.

"I guess food can wait." He tossed the laminated sheet to the floor and let his Domme get to work. She seemed more eager than usual. "Goddess?"

"Yes?" She continued with her intricate tie around his wrists.

"Are you happy? With me?"

"What?" She stopped and stared at him in surprise. "Is tha—do you think I'm not happy?"

"I just want to be sure. You make me happy, and I love being with you. I want to be sure you feel the same." Nervousness stirred in his stomach.

"Bash, baby." Gwen put her hands on either side of his face. "I love you. You make me *very* happy, and if you decided to move your life here, I would come with you, if that's what you wanted."

"Oh. Well." A silly smile spread across his face.

"Idiot." She nipped his bottom lip. "Now, do you want me to tie you up or not?"

"Please, my Goddess." Sebastian laid back on the bed and thought about the possibility of a life there with her while she carefully bound his arms and legs. *Oh, shit! I forgot it.* He held his sigh in and told himself to enjoy the moment regardless. *There'll be plenty of other chances.* "I love you, too," he said when she placed the blindfold over his eyes.

"My Knight."

"Yes?"

"I need you to say it for me."

"Please, put the headphones on. I surrender myself into your very capable hands. Ymroddi." Sebastian felt her slip them on and everything became muffled. The music started low and soft, slowly rising in volume until it was all he could hear. He was nervous at first, but with Gwen's fingertips caressing his skin and the smell of her lotion under the salt and tanning oil, he relaxed. *This isn't so bad. Don't know what I was worried about.*

Gwen checked the ties and kept an eye on his body language. Sebastian didn't seem aware he was nodding off, and she couldn't bring herself to keep him awake. She knew the holidays had been stressful and he'd done nothing but worry about work his brother could easily handle. Something deeper was on his mind. Gwen trusted Sebastian would tell her when he was ready, until then, she made him safe in her care. A small snore broke the silence, and she stifled a laugh before remembering he wouldn't hear it anyway. "Still so adorable, my Knight." She settled in next to him with her book, taking frequent breaks to ensure he was all right.

Sebastian awoke much later to find himself free of his restraints and Gwen asleep in the dark next to him. A loud rumble outside pulled his attention to the balcony, and a sharp flash of lightning revealed the door was still open. He jumped up and closed it as the rain began pelting against the glass.

"Bash?" Gwen's voice was thick with sleep, and she snuggled against him as he crawled back under the covers and wrapped his arms around her. "You're awake."

"Yeah. Why'd you let me fall asleep?"

"You were so comfortable and exhausted. That was the first time you've completely relaxed since Christmas. It was good for you." Gwen turned in his arms and draped a leg over his waist. "I'm glad you got some sleep. Is that thunder?"

"Mhm. We're in for quite a storm." He ran a hand along her leg, noticing she'd changed into one of her short, strappy nightgowns.

"What are you doing?" Gwen smiled in the dark when his hand moved further up.

"Well, I'm still very relaxed, but I didn't get to enjoy your company as much as I wanted. And when we were on the beach you did tell me I could continue my endeavors later. It's later." He trailed kisses along her neck and shoulder.

"That it is." Gwen pressed her hips against his as he slipped his fingers into her. She wrapped her hand behind his head, pulling him closer for a kiss and running her tongue along his. The small sound of enjoyment that came out of him made her want him more. "Take those things off. What did you call them before?"

"Boardies?"

"Yeah, that." She laughed. Sebastian kept trying to teach her some of the idioms of his home, but sometimes she just wanted to hear him say it instead. "Dych chi'n giwt."

"What'd you say?" He was halfway through tugging his shorts down but stopped to tickle her instead.

"I said 'you're cute'." She giggle-snorted and squirmed. "Ok, ok! If you don't take off your *boardies*, I'm going back to sleep."

"Yes, Goddess." Sebastian fumbled around to get them off while she finished catching her breath. He knew her sides would still be sensitive, so he was careful when he slid his hands up her body and pulled her nightgown off. The rain picked up outside. His beard scuffed against her skin as he kissed along her stomach; Sebastian cupped her breasts, savoring both before moving to nibble her ear. "Have I been good enough?"

"Enough for?"

"Ah...I can't take everything off by myself."

"Huh?" She pushed her hips against his again and felt metal. "Oh." *My bad.* "Well, I don't know," she snickered. "Why don't you ask me nicely."

Sebastian groaned. "Oh, glorious, merciful, gracious Goddess. The meaning of my existence. The breath in my body. Love of my life. Please release me from my cage."

"Why?" She bit her lip and tried not to sound too excited.

"Because I want to use every means available to pleasure you until the sun rises again." He nuzzled her neck. "And I need to be... *uncaged* to do that."

"That's a good argument. But where oh where did I put that key?"

"I might've spotted it on the nightstand."

"Of course, you did." She snagged the key. "How about a kiss first?"

"Anything you want, Love." Sebastian kissed Gwen deeply, breath catching when she reached down, unlocked the cage, and slipped it off. "Oh, Goddess. Thank you."

"You know the rules." Gwen pushed her hips into him to roll him over, but he didn't budge. "Sebastian?"

"May I break the rules tonight?" He felt her tense beneath him while she considered what he was asking. "May I give myself to you like this?"

"All right." Trust went both ways, and she needed to trust him not to take advantage. Bondage was easy, love was the hard part. Gwen allowed Sebastian to bury himself inside her. At first, he was hesitant; even when he was on top it was always a means of pleasing her. She could tell when he found his stride and bit her lip. No rules meant he could focus only on his needs if he wanted. She moaned when he changed tactics and pulled back to tease her gently with his tip.

"Goddess. My Goddess." Sebastian continued to tease her with light strokes, building anticipation for them both until they were panting. He wrapped one hand in her hair and put his other arm under her waist, using the leverage to sink deeper. Gwen felt her toes curl at the sudden sensation of having all of him and sighed into his kiss. "Will you come for me?"

"Harder." Her voice was quiet and breathless.

"You're so wonderful." Sebastian tightened his arm around her hips and thrust harder. Although he didn't need to wait for permission to come tonight, he held back for her. "Gwen," he moaned, ready to burst. "I need you."

"Tell me you love me." She trembled on the edge.

"I love you."

"I—" Gwen gasped as she came. A few seconds later, he joined her, relishing his own orgasm, and emptying himself into her. Sebastian trembled against her. "I love you, too," she said when she had the breath to speak again. They grew quiet for a while, and she thought maybe he'd fallen back asleep.

"That was selfish of me," Sebastian said into her neck.

"You're allowed to be selfish sometimes." She played with his fingers that were still wrapped in her hair. "Go to sleep."

"Mm. Not yet."

"What's wrong?"

"Nothing," he said with a grin. "I'm just, you know, getting my second wind."

"Is that so?" Gwen rolled her eyes. "Well, what if I'm tired?"

"Please?" A flash of lightning revealed pleading, puppy dog eyes. "My Goddess need only lie back and allow me to worship her." He dipped his head down to tease one of her breasts and wiggled his hips suggestively.

"I don't think you're going to get any deeper than that," she laughed.

"Oh, I'm going to have to beg to differ."

"Beg all you want. You know it turns me on when you do." Gwen let out a little whimper when he moved his attention to her other breast while he pulled out of her. "Where are you going?"

"I thought you were tired."

"Maybe, but I didn't want you to go anywhere."

"I think we're going to need a few things, but I need to see when they stop room service."

"*Now* you're hungry?"

"I'm always hungry when it comes to you." Sebastian lifted the forgotten menu from the floor and turned the light on low. "Ah, good, they're still taking orders. Anything you want?"

"Uh...dimmies."

"I'm afraid that's not an option, but we can go out tomorrow and see about getting some."

"Fine." She sighed dramatically. "Why don't we get something light? Otherwise, we'll just end up falling asleep."

"You know...we have food here. It's not going to be particularly fancy or filling—or healthy—but it's something, and then we wouldn't have to worry about being interrupted by room service."

Gwen rolled onto her side and propped herself up. "But I want some fancy room service."

"But room service doesn't have dimmies or Tim Tams or Cherry Ripes or some...Chilli Cheese Shapes."

"Sh...shapes? What are Shapes?"

"A snack."

"You're a snack," she said, stretching. "What about those blackcurrant and passionfruit drinks?"

"Picked them up already."

"Hm...can we have both?"

"You want room service *and* snackies?"

"Why not?"

"Well." He leaned down to kiss her shoulder. "We're going to need to refuel anyway."

"I think I see where this is going." She snuggled up under the blanket and listened to the storm outside while he made their order. "Wake me when it gets here. I have a feeling this is going to be a long vacation, and I want to be conscious for all of it."

8

Surrender

February 14th

Sebastian went over the details again carefully. He was armed with supplies for the night and everything on his to-do list was complete, but his nerves still refused to calm. This was his first Valentine's Day with Gwen, and they both wanted it to be special. When he'd brought the holiday up in the hopes of getting some ideas of what she'd like, Gwen interrupted him with an idea of her own that left him speechless. Her gift to him? For one night, they would switch. Tonight, Sebastian was the Dom, she would play the role of submissive, and he knew he was over-thinking the whole thing. This was his Gwen, his love and closest companion, not a stranger, and he had no reason to be so anxious. Sebastian took another look around his loft and checked his watch; he was ready with time to spare, but she was always a little early. There was a half-knock at the door, followed by keys in the lock.

"That smells lovely," Gwen said as she walked in and shut the door behind her.

"And it'll taste lovely." For a moment, he wasn't quite sure what to do. This was when he usually took her bag, helped her settle, asked what she wanted for dinner, and offered to rub her feet. *What am I supposed to do next?* Gwen's dark hair cascaded to her waist in soft waves, something he requested for their evening. Although she wasn't wearing anything meant to convey "Domme," her relaxed, confident posture still declared it, and he struggled with the temptation to revert to their usual dynamic. *Get it together. You're in charge tonight.* "I hope you're hungry, but first I want you to change. Your outfit for the evening is in the bathroom."

"All right." She tossed her bag on the couch and headed for the bathroom.

"Wait."

"Yes?"

"Tonight, I want you to call me, um…my Dear." *Damn it that doesn't sound dominant at all. She's going to laugh.*

"If that's what you desire."

"Oh." Sebastian stood dumbfounded for a moment. "Nah yeah, that's—I mean, yes, that's what I want. Now, g-g…get dressed." He shoved down the urge to say please. While she confined herself to change, he checked dinner and adjusted the place settings. *She's taking longer than I expected. Maybe she doesn't like it? Should have picked a different color.* He glared down at the made-from-scratch vodka sauce and mumbled another "damn it."

"Well?" Gwen's sudden appearance made him jump.

"Wow." The gauzy baby doll stopped halfway down her hips and left little to his imagination.

"What do you think?" She smoothed the pale blue fabric and adjusted the satin ribbon keeping it together.

"You look amazing."

"Thank you, my Dear."

"So, before we start, your safe word. Uh…w-what did you choose?"

"Multipass."

"I—what?"

"Mul. Ti. Pass."

"Tease. Don't talk nerdy to me unless you mean it."

"I always mean it." Gwen pecked him on the cheek.

"Uh huh. Sit." Sebastian gestured to the couch before casually wiping at his mouth. Seeing her in something so delicately feminine was strange, but the sight of her curves had the same effect as always, as did the click of fluff-adorned heels across the laminate floor. "I have something else for you to wear," he said, giving the sauce a final stir and turning off the stove. *The noodles can wait.* Sebastian forced himself to slow down as he walked behind her to the couch. He grabbed a small, black box from the coffee table and presented it to her. "Open it."

"A collar?" Gwen lifted it from the box, examining the rows of diamonds.

"You don't like it?" He wanted to smack himself. *That wasn't a Dom's response.*

"I like it if you like it. Do you want me to wear it?"

"Yes." He nodded mostly to reassure himself and set the box back down. "Ok, here we go." Sebastian's hands shook a little as he raised the glittering collar to her neck. It felt strange to be in charge, a little wrong, and his fingers fumbled with the clasp. She held her dark hair out of the way and waited patiently. His breath whooshed out when the pieces finally slid into place. "Beautiful."

"Thank you." Gwen sat with her hands folded in her lap. "What now, my Dear?"

"Uh." He knew she was trying to be encouraging without taking over his scene, it was her nature to be helpful, and he appreciated the little nudges to keep going. "May I...I mean, dance with me." He clicked a button, and a soft waltz swayed out of the speakers. Sebastian set the remote down and gently pulled Gwen from the couch. Ballroom dancing wasn't one of his strong suits, but he enjoyed it and wanted to share that with her. The frilly baby doll fluttered as he twirled her around the loft, and the material kept coming open below the ribbon tied under her breasts. He knew it was supposed to do that, but it was distracting. Sebastian licked his lips at the sight of her bare curves and the sheer, blue panties before slipping his hand under the gauze. "Your skin is always so soft," he murmured. He tugged her against him and took the kiss he wanted. She was warm and inviting, giving. *But something's missing. This is my Goddess, but....* He brushed aside the uncertainty trying to undermine his confidence and went back to dancing, leading her through the next two songs while he thought about what should be next. A small growl came from his stomach. "Dinner, right. We should eat."

"If that's what you want, my Dear. But may I ask something?"

"Um. Yes?" They stopped dancing and he noticed they were closer to the bed than the kitchen. *I wonder how much nicer that outfit would look on the floor.*

"Will you kiss me again?" She fluttered her lashes at him sweetly.

"Such a tease." Sebastian smirked. The kiss was supposed to be light, a promise of more to come after dinner, but she smelled so good, and the bed was so close. He wrapped her legs around his waist to carry her the short distance to paradise. "You're so beautiful." Her shoes clattered to the floor as Sebastian tumbled her onto the bed and covered her with kisses. The ribbon tore when he started pulling at it, so he gave up being gentle and ripped the rest of the outfit away, but he left the collar on and pushed her back. "Undo my belt, Love."

"Yes, Dear." She did as she was told while he unbuttoned his shirt and tossed it aside.

"Say your mine, Gwen." He worked his slacks off and climbed onto the bed with her.

"I'm yours." She responded to his demanding kisses by giving.

"Only mine?" He bit her shoulder lightly and thought about how much he wanted her.

"Yes, only yours."

"Good. I want you."

"Then take me."

When he slipped a finger under the diamond collar and gently tugged her up to nip her bottom lip, she followed. His other hand roamed her bare body, searching until he found what he wanted, but her words and attitude stuck in his mind. Sebastian thought about the way she said it—"take me"—and stopped. *Gwen never talks like that. She hates that phrase.* "I…. No. This isn't right." Sebastian let go of the collar and looked down at her helplessly. She looked beautiful under him, but everything was wrong. "I can't be…this. Gingerbread, Gwen. Gingerbread."

"Can't play Dom?" She laughed and stroked his cheek. "Not quite how you imagined it would be?"

"No, it's not. Don't get me wrong, I love touching and pashing you as much as I want, and dancing with you was wonderful, but I also love the rules. I need the rules."

"What about when I let you break them?"

"Those are rare exceptions, and I still put you first. My goal is always to please you. I can't just switch that around and be in control.

You come first. Always." He nuzzled her hand. "*I* submit to *you*, not the other way around."

"You don't want to finish after all your hard work to put this together?"

"No. I need you to permit me to be myself." Sebastian kissed her palm and rubbed his face into it. "Please, Goddess. Will you be my Domme?"

"Of course."

"If I might make a suggestion?"

"Hm?" She nodded for him to continue.

"Let's eat dessert first."

"Are you all right to keep going right now? We can take a break, have some dinner. There's no need to rush."

"No, I'm fine, I want to keep going, as long as you're my Domme." He ran his hands over her body. "As long as I get to submit to you."

"You're sure?"

"Yeah, Love, I'm sure. Please, I need this. I need to be..."

"I understand, Bash. Come here." Gwen grabbed his chin gently as he leaned down and kissed him. "You want your dessert first?"

"Please."

"Mm I think that's allowable. Now," she arched her hips into his. "Be a good boy and please me."

"Yes, Goddess." He closed his eyes while she stroked his erection, making him harder. "What may I do for you this evening?"

"This." Gwen widened her legs and guided him in. "That's a good boy."

"The collar," he said around unsteady breaths as she rubbed against him.

"It's not a collar. It's a beautiful necklace you bought me for Valentine's Day. Do you want to be my Valentine, my Knight?"

"Please."

"Good. I have something for you, too."

"But you already gave me somethi—" He gasped when she tightened around him. "Fuck."

"Such a handsome boy. You're so cute when you make that face." She giggled when his cheeks flushed bright red. "And you're my handsome boy, aren't you?"

"Y...yes."

"Do you want to come?"

"Yes, please."

"Then tell me you love me."

"I love you, Goddess." Sebastian moaned as she quickened the pace. "Please, may I come? Please?"

"Yes."

He buried his face in the curve of her neck and moaned her name while he came. "Thank you, Goddess."

"I love you, too, Bash. You're such a good boy." Gwen played with his hair and kissed his cheek, waiting for him to stop shaking.

"Let's not ever stop being us, Love." Sebastian wrapped his arms around her and nuzzled as close as he could get. He loved aftercare with Gwen.

"What do you mean?"

"I want to be yours forever, your sub, your partner. And I want you to be my Domme forever, my partner. Let's never try to change that or let anyone else change it."

"Ok," she said and restrained a laugh at how quickly "the cuddles," as she'd decided to call it, had taken over him. "I didn't think you were that deep in your subspace already, Bash. Why didn't you say anything?"

"No, no, I like it. I feel I can be completely open with you, no boundaries, no secrets. That's how I want to be with you. All the time." He rolled them onto their sides so he could bring his knees up until the pair of them were wrapped up in each other completely. "I just want us to...be happy together and not do anything unless it makes us happy. We have our way of doing it, and it's perfect and wonderful."

"Bash?"

"Hm?" He was already half asleep.

"Is...." She sighed and amended her original question. "What do you need right now?

"Just being here with you is enough."

"You're shaking," Gwen said, massaging his thigh to soothe the nerves.

"I'm sorry. I'm just so...so...blissfully drained. It's like...like...uhm...."

"Being high on something?

"Nah yeah. Fabian joked it's like a truth serum because you could ask me anything right now, and I'll just tell you." He wriggled his shoulders around a little, so he was able to see her face. He wanted Gwen to see his vulnerability and openness. He trusted her to keep him safe. "Ask me anything, my Goddess, anything."

After a long moment of consideration, she said, "the other week, you mentioned collaring and the different types and meanings that go with it. Why?"

"Because I want you to collar me, Goddess. I want to be owned by you, and I want the world to know it. And I'm not going anywhere. You are where I belong."

"I see. A real collar then. You're completely committed?"

"Ydw, dw i'n ymroddhi i chi." *Yes, I surrender to you.* "Did I say it right?"

"Yes, you said it perfectly. When you're leveled out again, we'll discuss it more."

"I love you and never want this to change."

"I love you, too, Bash. We'll unwind a bit, and then you need to eat something. You're still shakier than I like."

"Ok." Sebastian dozed off while she continued playing with his hair. *This is where I belong, this is home. Choosing to submit to Gwen is one of the best decisions I've ever made.* "Will you be my Valentine, Goddess?"

"Of course. And when we're all good here, we'll have some food, and you can see my gift for you."

"You still got me something else?"

"Mhm."

"Well, that necklace is actually yours, if you're ok with that. I saw it in a window when I was walking down Fifth Ave and thought it would be so beautiful on you."

"You have good taste, Bash." She gave him a small squeeze and kissed his forehead.

"They're real. Real diamonds," he clarified.

"I'll have to make sure I save it for special occasions, so it doesn't get dirty."

"There's a warranty. We can get it fixed if something happens."

"My prudent planner."

"Thank you."

"For what?

"For allowing me to be here and share a life with you, Gwen. Allowing me to submit to you. Tonight, I'm totally certain my place is at your feet. I can and will only ever surrender to you, my Goddess." Sebastian mumbled something else that ended in a light snore.

"So devoted. My handsome Knight." She kissed his head again and let him sleep.

9

Submission

Early March

Wisteria and jasmine drifted over Sebastian while his Domme slowly scraped her nails down his chest and stomach. He shivered at the sensation. His craving for Gwen made his mouth water. Whenever the blindfold went on, it created an instant need, a deep physical desire to be touched by her. His jeans were getting tight, but she knew his body well by now and was already tugging the zipper down before he could get uncomfortable. He instinctively clenched his fists, which were suspended over his head while he stood shirtless in the kitchen. Vaguely, he wondered how she'd managed to hang the rope.

"My, you're so big already. Have you been thinking about me today?" Gwen knew he couldn't answer around the gag. He moaned out something incoherent when she knelt to run her tongue along his cock. "Tsk, tsk. You shouldn't speak with a full mouth." She smiled and adjusted the ties, making sure the bar keeping his ankles apart was secure. "Now, about that bit of cheek the other day...." The mat usually in front of her throne looked perfect under his feet as Gwen continued to lick and stroke. When he was close to coming, she stopped.

Sebastian wisely kept the rest of his noises to himself; this was his punishment for sassing her at the end of their previous session.

"Good boy," she said, petting his head and enjoying the sincerity on his face as he nuzzled her hand.

Gwen had been waiting for him when he got home from work, dressed in a black corset that left her breasts exposed and sharp, strappy heels that matched. The next moments were a blur: the front door locked, his satchel tossed on the couch, his shirt stripped off. Sebastian barely remembered being restrained. Her unusually aggressive dominance put him in his subspace almost instantly, and he relished the denial almost as much as he needed the release. There would be a bit of begging ahead of him if he wanted to come tonight. She lightly smacked his ass with her riding crop once. Before the second one came, he flinched.

"Hm." Instead of following through with the agreed-upon three, she loosened the tie holding his arms up.

Part of Sebastian wanted to protest. He'd agreed to the punishment, but his Domme removed the spreader bar and tugged him along.

"Sit." Gwen watched him get on his knees silently before sitting in her chair. She crossed her legs, trying not to think about how wet she was, and set a plain black box in her lap. "I have something for you, but I'm not sure if you *really* want it." Silence. She removed the ball gag. "You may speak now."

"Please, Goddess, I want it," he said, licking his lips quickly and working his jaw a bit now that his mouth was free. "I'll be good. Anything you want. Please." Sebastian was a captive groveling at the feet of a fierce warrior queen. One wrong move and she might lock him in the dungeon. Or not let him get off. He was so turned on by this play he was close to coming at the thought of pleasuring her with his tongue. "Let me service you, my Goddess. Let me worship you."

"I don't know. I'm not sure you've earned it." Gwen took the blindfold off and so he could see the box.

"What is it?" Sebastian eyed it intently.

"Something important. Something only a devoted sub deserves." She removed the top of the box and pulled out a black leather collar tooled in a masculine, Celtic knot pattern. A silver plate was bolted to it with "My Knight" etched into the metal. Collaring was something he'd expressed an interest in, and they'd discussed it at length already. At first, she was hesitant, but Sebastian assured her he was serious.

Gwen spent more than a month searching for the right one, and nearly another month waiting for it to arrive. Sebastian sat a little straighter at her feet. "Do you think you've earned this?"

"I try to be worthy of you, Goddess, but only you decide if I am."

"Do you want it?"

"Yes, Goddess. Please." He wanted that collar, to feel the leather caressing his neck while she tied him down and fucked him.

"I'm not convinced yet," she said as a slow smile crept across her burgundy lips.

"How can I persuade you?" Sebastian had his suspicions, but the game was too much fun to preempt her order.

"Be a good boy and beg."

"Please," he began, bowing his head, "please, I want it. I'll do anything to be owned by you, Goddess, anything you desire."

"Say it again."

"Plea—"

"Just the last part."

"I'll do anything to be owned by you, Goddess, anything you desire."

"Mm. Perfect." She shifted around in her chair to move closer, then stopped. "There's one more thing I want to hear, if you're serious about this."

"I submit to you completely, my Goddess." He knew exactly what she wanted. "Dw i'n ymroddi i chi." Sebastian heard the metallic clink of the buckles as they came undone. The scent of new leather mixed with her perfume, and he bit his lip against the groan that wanted to escape at the sensation of the collar on his skin. His body throbbed with need for her.

"That looks quite handsome on you," she said, leaning back. The black stood out well against his skin, and the curve of leather looked scrumptious against his scruffy jawline, which she very much wanted to lick. But her sub's punishment wasn't quite done. A second box sat on the end table next to her. "I want you to watch now."

"Yes, Goddess." Sebastian swallowed hard when his Domme spread her legs; she hadn't been wearing any panties the entire time, and so far, he'd done well not thinking about it. His cock twitched in anticipation. Gwen slid a hand down her pale breasts, teasing her nipples as she went, and started stroking herself. He imagined how she tasted and recalled the last time she'd let him eat her. Her fingers paused, and he leaned forward just a little.

"Hungry, are we?" She flipped the lid off the other box on the end table next to her and pulled out a blue vibrator. Free of the packaging and armed with a fresh charge, the toy was ready to work. Gwen put it to the lowest setting and leaned down to press it against his cock and balls. She watched his lids flutter closed and hands clench before giggling and moving it away. When he opened his eyes, she made sure he saw everything. Her fingers worked inside while the toy teased her clit. Slowly, they switched, and she slid the vibrator in place. She widened her legs and draped one over the arm of the chair so Sebastian could have a better view, then turned the toy up several notches as she worked it in and out, faster, then slower, and then faster again. Gwen watched her sub stare enviously and hungrily while she edged herself to punish him. He wanted so badly to have her. "Don't you look handsome in your new collar," she panted.

"Thank you, Goddess." Sebastian stayed focused. He couldn't decide what he wanted more: to lick her until she came in his mouth or be mounted and fucked on the floor. The toy taunted him as it slid in and out, humming happily. Gwen used her other hand to rub her breasts and tease her nipples again. He knew she was close to orgasm.

"Come here." She motioned him closer and wrapped her hand around the back of his neck, pressing his face to her stomach while she kept going with the vibrator. "I want your tongue where it'll do the most good."

"As it pleases you," he said, voice muffled against the smooth corset. Sebastian tasted her on the toy when he started working and tried to time his licks with her strokes. The hum made his tongue tingle, but he was happy to finally be allowed to serve his Domme. She came and made him stop, but he knew she wasn't satisfied. Gwen always got a little half-smirk when she was truly pleased. "What's wrong, Goddess?"

"I think you've been punished enough for tonight." She put the toy aside and produced a matching leash from the first box to clip onto his collar. "Follow," she said as she got up and gave it a little tug. Sebastian had no choice but to scramble to his feet and trot after her toward the bed, pants half-falling to his knees on the way. Gwen stripped off the rest of his clothes and made him get on the bed where she secured his still-bound wrists to a metal ring he'd screwed to the headboard for such occasions. She shortened her grip on the leash and pulled gently as she leaned close enough to run her tongue across his lips. "Are you ready for me?"

"Yes, Goddess." Her eyes were dark and hungry. The feeling of being owned and dominated by Gwen was as intoxicating as the smell of leather, wisteria, and jasmine.

"Hold this." She placed the end of the leash in his mouth and made him bite down, which was just as well because it helped him stave off his orgasm when she slid onto his cock. Gwen rocked her hips against her sub, starting deep and giving him no relief. She didn't need to speak. He knew his place. Sebastian in his subspace was always a delight for her to watch because he let his usual restraints fall away. The trust and love she saw in his face in that moment made her slow the pace; she said his punishment for the night was over, and his body told her he was at his limit. "Come for me, my Knight." Gwen wondered if she'd held him back too long, but, like a good sub, he came only when she did. She huffed out a breath, finally allowing the exhaustion of the day to sink in and unbound him.

"Thank you, Goddess." He closed his eyes contentedly while she rubbed his wrists. "Do I get to keep the collar on?"

"Yes, but that leash is coming off. I don't want you to get tangled in it while we're sleeping."

"Mmkay." Sebastian's stomach growled. "Can we order out tonight and watch a moooviiieee?"

"You sound like a dork when you say it that way." She snorted and rolled to the side so he could sit up.

"That's the point." He followed her when she rolled and stole a kiss. "I'm only comfortable being a dork with you and my brother."

"Good." She nuzzled his nose and sighed.

"What would you like me to order for you?" *There it is,* he thought as the half-smirk appeared. "We haven't had pizza in a while."

"That sounds good." Gwen felt him get out of bed and started to drift off, listening to him shuffle through his drawers for something to wear. "Do you want to shower?"

"As long as I get to put this back on." She didn't have to look to know he was pointing to the collar. "I don't want to get it wet."

"Mhm. I got you a day collar, too, but I'll give it to you in the morning."

"Ok." He shuffled off happily to order and get the water ready for their shower. "It'll be about an hour, so we have time. Are you falling asleep?"

"No."

"Sure, you aren't," he teased before lifting her into his lap. Sebastian sat patiently while his Domme took the leather from around his neck. Without it, he felt more naked. It was a sense of absence he couldn't quite put into words yet as Gwen set his collar on the nightstand.

"Shall we?"

"Yes." He carried her into the bathroom. Hot water poured over them, invigorating him again, and he decided tonight he'd do a little more than wash his Goddess. Pulling her damp hair gently out of the way, Sebastian nuzzled the crook of her neck and nibbled her ear. "I need you."

"Do you now?" Gwen turned to face him and saw he was hard again. "I guess you *were* thinking about me all day. What do you say when you want something from your Goddess?"

"Please? Pretty please?" A nod and a small smile were all the encouragement he needed. Sebastian lifted her against the tile wall and buried himself in her, thrusting hard with her legs wrapped around his waist. "Hnh. Gwen, baby, I am so damn crazy about you." He desperately wanted to see that half-smirk again.

"I'm...crazy...about you too, Bash." She dug her nails into his wet back as she came. "Fuck."

"Will you come for me again?" He kept going until she did before he allowed himself release. "Gwen, You're amazing." Sebastian nuzzled her neck, covering it with sweet kisses, and let her back down so they could finish their shower.

"I'm just me."

"And *you* are amazing." Sebastian stuck his tongue out at her, not caring if he got punished again. The expression he caught wasn't the one he'd been hoping for. "What's wrong, Love? Did I hurt you?"

"No, it's just been a horribly long week." Gwen let him go back to washing her and tried to relax.

"Is that all?" he asked, voice soft. The tension wouldn't leave her body so he did the only thing he could think to and took care of her.

Sebastian turned the water off and grabbed a towel. When she was dry, he pulled one of his shirts over her head and walked her to the couch so they could sit while he combed her hair. *Something* was wrong, but he couldn't put his finger on what. Dinner came, and they watched one of her favorite movies. Still, she didn't relax. At bed, she held him a little tighter than usual, and he finally wrapped his arms around her. He needed an answer. "Please, tell me what's bothering you." Sebastian felt her sigh more than he heard it.

"I'm worried I got carried away earlier."

"What? Why would you think that?"

"I know you don't like spanking, Bash. When you flinched, I decided it was better to stop than follow through with the rest." Gwen squeezed a little tighter. "And I hadn't planned to be so…. I don't know what came over me."

"Are you kidding? Ok, I admit I'm not a fan of being spanked, but you were punishing me, and I told you I would accept within reason. Three was more than reasonable. But that aggressiveness is a whole different story." She tensed in his arms, keeping her face hidden against his chest. "Gwen, Love, that was hot. Really, *really* hot. I'm still turned on thinking about it, but that's neither here nor there. You didn't get carried away, and you didn't hurt me. I enjoyed our session immensely."

"Are you sure?"

"Absolutely." Sebastian rubbed her back gently and waited for her to look up at him. "Please don't cry," he said when he saw her amber eyes were rimmed with red.

"I can't help it. I'm just emotional right now for some reason, and I just…. I don't know. But I'm the Domme. I should always know."

"You know you don't always have to be on top of everything. It's ok to let those things go sometimes and not get worked up about them." Sebastian watched her roll off the bed and make a grab for her comb again, but he beat her to it. She was clearly upset about more. "Goddess," he said calmly as he coaxed her back onto the bed, "why don't we have a serious conversation about the session and the dynamics of our relationship? We can talk about what did or didn't work in the session, see if any we've found any new personal limits, or if some old ones are a little less rigid than before. But." He paused for emphasis and went back to fixing her hair. "We can only do it if we're both calm and collected."

"That might help, I guess." She rubbed her hands over her face.

"In fact, I've something we can do to lead up to that and maybe it'll help up to figure out what's wrong." Sebastian finished her hair with a braid and stretched across the bed to pull his forest-green journal from his nightstand. "I'll write about our session tonight in my journal, the way I perceived it all. And I know your journal isn't here, but I have plenty of paper and pens, so you can write about our session from your point of view."

"I did bring it, actually. It's in my bag." Gwen sighed. *How can I tell him?* "Bash, baby. I…"

"You can tell me anything," he said, moving to twine his fingers with hers. "I'm here for you."

"I lost my job today. Nine years of giving them everything and pouring myself into every project so it would be as close to perfect as possible, and this, *this* is my reward." Gwen wiped at the tears as the stress she'd been avoiding finally overtook her. "They didn't even give me a good reason, just some bullshit about the company deciding to move in a different direction. What the hell does that even mean?"

"I'm so sorry, Love." Sebastian pulled her back into him carefully and cuddled her. "It's going to be ok though. I promise."

"How though? How am I supposed to be a proper Domme and take care of you? I'm so weak I can't hang on to a job. No job means no money to pay bills or buy you nice things or…or…" All the pent-up frustration and anguish threatened to choke her.

"Gwen, my Goddess, you know that I don't need material things to know you care. What's more, you've only been responsible for your own bills, apart from the membership fees for the club, which are for both of us. You're smart. I know you've saved some money, so, if you're ok with it, we can take some time tomorrow and go over your finances to come up with a plan." He kissed her forehead and wiped the tears away. "I promise you everything will be ok. I'm here to help you and serve you. Whatever you need, we can make it happen."

"Bash…." Gwen pouted a little, still swimming in her misery. "Ok. Yeah, ok. Let's do that tomorrow, but tonight I *do* want to journal about our session. I think that's a good idea, especially since this was different from our usual play nights." She jumped down from the bed and walked quickly to her own bag sitting on Sebastian's dresser.

Gwen came back with her peacock-blue notebook and silver fountain pen.

"Ready to write?" He held out a hand to help her on the bed.

"I love you, Bash." She settled next to him and opened to a blank page about three-quarters of the way in.

"R...rwy'n dy garu du, Gwen." The happy surprise that lit up her face was well-worth a little stuttering to get it right.

"You've been practicing!" She jumped into his lap and wrapped her arms around him, before kissing him deeply and without restraint. "It's so sexy when you say it like that, Bash, makes me want to keep pashin' on you."

"Mm. Good," he said around kisses, "I suppose we can write later."

"Say it again, my Knight."

"Rwy'n dy garu du, my Goddess." Journals momentarily forgotten, Sebastian was happy to find creative ways of pleasing his Goddess until she fell asleep with that satisfied, half-smirk on her face.

10

Cherished

April 19th

Gwen opened the door to her apartment and stepped in from the dim hallway. Her kitchen was quiet and lit only by the light over the stove. Sebastian had asked her to let him do something special tonight, since it was the anniversary of their first session, and she wondered what he'd planned. She sniffed the air as she locked the door and smiled—it smelled like cookies. A plate of little Gingerbread Men sat on the kitchen table with a note. Gwen nibbled on a cookie and read Sebastian's message: check the fridge. "So, it's a scavenger hunt? You're so cute, Bash."

She hung her satchel on a chair and went to the fridge. "Oh ho ho. Someone's breaking out the good stuff." An expensive bottle of rosé champagne sat on the middle shelf next to a pair of elegant, crystal flutes and another note.

Check your desk.

This is fun. The living room was dotted with vases of lavender roses and flickering candles of various sizes. Her desk was covered in a smattering of rose petals surrounding a little piece of paper on top of a long, narrow black box.

I hope you like it.

"Welp." Gwen had to set the champagne and glasses down to

open the box, which had a delicate bracelet with several silver charms inside. "A key, handcuffs, a kangaroo...a gingerbread man...a... what's," she squinted. "*Oh*, it's a tiny cat's paw tie!" She clipped the bracelet on and opened the note tucked into the lid of the box.

The bookcase, your favorite color.

Only two books in her collection were the same peacock blue she loved—her current journal and an old one filled with her poetry, regrets, and dreams. Sebastian was the only person she trusted to read it without judgment. Another note was tucked between the pages bookmarking his favorite entry, and on it was a little poem of his own.

My place or yours
Here or abroad
Wherever you are
Is where I belong
I want to worship you always
And bask in your love
But I'm not good at this clue-thing
Please meet me in the tub

Gwen rolled her eyes and snorted. "Dork." The bathroom was just down the hall, between the living room and bedroom, and the door to the latter was suspiciously closed. She walked into the short hallway, turned to the off-white bathroom door, and nudged it open. "My, oh, my. What have we here?"

"My Goddess." Sebastian sat on the edge of her claw foot tub, shirtless, loofah in hand. "May I offer you a hot bath?"

"Most definitely." Several small candles placed strategically around the tight space provided the only light beyond the dim glow of evening coming through the little window. Bubbles filled the tub and sparkled blue in the candlelight.

"Allow me." Sebastian set the loofah down to take the champagne and set it to the side with the glasses. "I thought you might enjoy a drink with your bath." Slowly, he removed her boots and socks, unzipped her trousers, and tugged off her burgundy sweater. He kissed his way along her shoulders as he removed her bra, then down her stomach while he slid her panties to the floor.

"You're very affectionate tonight." Gwen took the hand he offered, climbed into the tub, and let the warmth envelope her. "Mm. I definitely needed this."

"Of course. You worked hard this week. I'm proud of you for putting yourself back out there, even if nothing's happened yet. I have absolute faith in you, my Goddess." Sebastian poured champagne into a glass and wrapped her fingers around the stem, kissing each knuckle before getting to work. His hand disappeared into the bubbles and emerged dripping with blueish water that he wrung from the loofah. For the next thirty minutes or so, he gently scrubbed her body, fingers occasionally taking a detour to tease her beneath the surface. When she was clean and relaxed, he pulled the stopper to let the water drain and helped her out. "Are you ready for your massage, my Goddess?"

"Mmhmm." Gwen finished her drink so she could hold the towel around herself and let him guide her to the bedroom. Like the bathroom and living room, there were candles throughout her room, but he'd added a path of white jasmine, purple wisteria, and deep red dahlia petals. A bouquet of lavender roses, heliotrope, and Queen Anne's lace sat on her nightstand in a black vase. Gwen knew every detail was significant right down to the flowers he'd chosen. *What is he up to?* "Attentive *and* romantic. I'm impressed."

"Oh…it gets better," he said with a sly smile as he walked her toward the bed. Once she was sitting, legs tucked to her side, he poured her another glass and joined her. Sebastian pumped a bit of detangler into his hands and massaged her scalp and neck before taking a black, wood comb from the nightstand to run through her long locks. His hands moved to her shoulders. "Would you like to lie down?"

"All right." She tried to read his features, but he kept his poker face up and only smiled reassuringly. *He's definitely up to something.* Gwen pulled the towel off, tossing it to the floor, and hugged the pillow already waiting for her as she laid down on the silver comforter.

Without needing to be told, Sebastian started with her lower back, where she was always the tensest, and moved up. She sighed into the pillow when he finished working out the knot between her shoulders. He worshipped her body slowly, beard scuffing against her skin as he trailed kisses along her spine and slipped one hand between her thighs. Strong fingers, slick from her arousal, stroked steadily until she moaned into the pillow. Sebastian pulled his hand back and rolled her over to kiss and massage the front of her body. "Will you let me prove my devotion to you tonight?"

"And how do you plan to do that?" Gwen smirked and admired the way his muscles looked in the flickering light. She watched as he undid his jeans and took them off before dipping his head down to leave another trail of kisses along one of her legs. When he nibbled her hip and slid his fingers back into her, she bit her lip and closed her eyes. Gwen reveled in the attention and care he took in making her feel good, and in his willingness to put off his own pleasure. Her hips arched, pushing into his hand. "Ask me for what you want."

"May I be inside you?" She nodded, and Sebastian thrust himself into her. She came after a few steady strokes. As intense as the sensation of her tightening around him was, he kept his pace consistent and made sure Gwen's hips were at the best angle. Her pleasure was his priority, and he needed to do everything right tonight. He knew he was when she orgasmed again. Having spent the entire day planning this night and thinking about his Domme naked, it was hard for him to hold back now. He started thrusting harder and felt her body shudder.

"Sebastian." She rarely said his name when they were playing.

"My Goddess," he said, voice quavering.

"Come for me."

"As it pleases you." He almost couldn't get the words out. Gwen tensed and moaned, and he let himself join his Goddess in her ecstasy. Sebastian waited until he was sure they were both done before he pulled away to collapse on the bed next to her. "Happy anniversary," he gasped as he tried to get his heart rate under control.

"Happy anniversary, Bash." Gwen rolled over and kissed him. "Thank you for taking such good care of me."

"Mm. I'm not quite done yet."

"Oh? Are you going to feed me some of those cookies, too?"

"I might." He chuckled and marveled in the sensation of her stretched out against him. Sebastian loved her apartment. It was cozier than his, and there wasn't a place Gwen's personality couldn't be felt. Sometimes he thought about asking if she wanted to move in together. *Maybe after this.* "But, before we get to food, would you close your eyes for just a moment?"

"All right." Gwen tilted her head questioningly but did as he asked. The mattress moved as he shifted around on the bed, rolling away then quickly turning back to face her. Whatever he was after hadn't been far.

"Gwen, my Goddess." Sebastian watched her eyes open and move from his face to the little blue box in his hand. It was wrapped in Tiffany's signature ribbon. He held his breath and the box while she undid the bow and looked inside. She bit her lip and met his eyes. "This is me. Asking for what I want. Will you allow me the honor of being your Knight for the rest of my life? Will you allow me to spend the rest of my life worshiping you, my Goddess? Will you let me love you always?"

"Sebastian." It took Gwen a moment to process what he was asking. An elegant, round solitaire glittered at her from within the box. Something about it scared her—bad memories—but when she looked back into his eyes, the fear disappeared. She almost couldn't find the words to reply. "Yes. Yes, I'll allow it!" She kissed him while he put the ring on.

"I'm so crazy about you, Gwen. You're everything to me."

"You're everything to me, too." She couldn't stop kissing him and basked in the glow of happiness wrapped up in his arms. *This is right. We're right.* "How long have you been planning this?"

"Um. Since…Chrissy…ish? New Year's seemed wrong, and then I thought about asking when we were on vacation, but I forgot to pack the ring." He kissed her forehead and gently ran his fingertips along her arm. "I asked Nate what he thought might be a properly special way to ask, and he suggested I do it on our 'kink-iversary,' as he called it."

"'Kink-iversary'?" Gwen snorted. "Your brother's such a dipstick, but that's a good name for it. And a great suggestion for a day. Your Goddess is *very* pleased. Happy Kink-iversary, my Knight."

"Happy Kink-iversary, my Goddess." He started to relax until her stomach grumbled.

"So…about those cookies."

"I promise we have more than cookies for dinner," Sebastian hugged Gwen closer.

"I didn't smell anything else."

"That's because I still have to make it."

"Oh." She pouted a little. "What is it?"

"Your favorite."

"Sushi?"

"Close." He chuckled when her eyes widened. "Yeah, I'm going to make your eel and rice."

"Yes!" Gwen bounced up on the bed and stumbled off. "Let's go."

"Coming, coming. But after, may I worship you some more?" He hoped he didn't look too excited.

Gwen smirked mischievously. "If you're a good boy." She ran out of the room, and he gave chase, eager to serve.

11

Everything Nice

October

Gwen smoothed the front of her white, silk robe and fidgeted in her chair. The stylist had already finished with her, but she still had close to an hour before it was time to put the dress on. *An hour of no touching my face or hair. I can't even lie down for a little bit. Ugh. What am I supposed to do? At least my nails are good to go.* She clicked her ombre blue nails together and giggled. "Rawr."

Woofwoof.

She picked up her phone. "Bash? Why's he texting me?"

Can you do something for me?

Is everything ok?

Yeah. I just need you to do something for me.

What do you need?

I know I'm not supposed to see you before the ceremony, but I need you.

Give me a minute. Blindfold yourself.

Thank you, Goddess.

She sent him a wink emoji and thought of something devious. *Oh, yes. That's perfect. Absolutely perfect.* "I should have some rope in here." They'd packed everything and brought their luggage with them to the wedding location so they could leave as soon as the reception was done, and she wasn't going to pass up the opportunity to spend their honeymoon dominating Sebastian in new and delectable ways. Gwen dug around one bag and pulled out a few lengths before sneaking into the hallway and a couple doors down to Sebastian's room.

"Come in," he said when she knocked.

"Don't you look scrumptious." She bit her lip at the sight of her husband-to-be. Sebastian sat patiently on the edge of the bed wearing nothing but black boxer-briefs, a white undershirt, and a silk tie covering his eyes. After locking the door, she set the rope on the comforter next to him and put her hands on his thighs. "Did you miss me last night, Bashie?"

"Yes." Sebastian stressed the word, groaning at the sensation of her hands caressing his chest before she ran her fingers through his hair. "I was miserable without you next to me."

"I missed you, too." Gwen opened her robe, revealing skin he couldn't see, and climbed into his lap, pushing her body against him. "Touch me."

"Yes, Goddess." He slid his hands along her bare legs obediently, then up her sides, stopping to cup her breasts and revel in the softness of her bare body. "Hm. No bra? May I?"

"You may." While his tongue teased her nipple, she closed her eyes in pleasure. "I have an idea for you."

"Please, tell me," he begged around kisses and licks.

"A rope harness. Under your tux." Gwen felt him getting harder.

"I love it." His laugh tickled her skin. "I love you."

"I love you, too, my Knight. Now," she said, reaching a hand down to slip his erection through the slit in his boxers. "Shall I be nice…or mean?"

"As it pleases you." Someone knocked, interrupting their moment. Sebastian growled in frustration. "Who is it?"

"Your brother. I'm making sure everything is all good. Do you need anything?"

"Grinnin' like a shot fox in here. Now, rack off. Please."

"Right," Nate said, disbelief in his voice. "And since I didn't get a response when I tried to check on her, I'm going to guess your blushing bride is in there with you."

"Don't worry, he can't see me." Gwen stifled a laugh at the aggravated sigh coming from the other side of the door. "I'm just making sure he's...dressed appropriately. And we both know you're the only one blushing here."

"Can't you two behave for just a few more hours?"

"Behave?" Sebastian snorted and went back to fondling his Domme. "Never heard of it."

"Is that so?" Gwen grabbed his chin and nipped at his bottom lip. "We'll see about that."

"You have forty-five minutes before you BOTH need to be dressed. *Try* not to miss your own wedding." Nate's muttering retreated, along with his footsteps.

"May I just say that I am looking forward to seeing you in that dress?" He worked his hands back down to Gwen's hips and pulled her a little closer. "I love pashin' you." Their lips brushed. He didn't think he could get any harder while she continued to fondle him, until she pressed against him, rubbing in time with her stroking. "Goddess." Sebastian's mind went blank.

"Confess to me, Knight. Tell me what you desire." She slid up until she could brush the tip of his throbbing cock so he could feel how wet she was.

"Hnh." He panted, completely focused on her scent and her body poised against him. "I...d...desire...you, Goddess."

"That's a good boy." Gwen mounted him and reveled in the pleasure of having him thick and hard inside her when she wanted him so badly. She savored every whimper from her sub and made him lie back as she edged them both toward orgasm. "Do you want to come for me?"

"Yes." Everything Sebastian wanted was on top of him, pushing his limits. His body shuddered. "Please, I need to come."

"Who's handsome boy are you?"

"Yours," he moaned softly, blushing.

"You're gonna wear your collar while I fuck you tonight."

"Anything you want."

"Beg. Beg me, baby."

Sebastian panted. "Ple-e...ease.... Please, Goddess, let me come."

"Mm. I love when you beg, Bash. Oh, fuck." She bit back her moan when she came—they didn't need the whole house hearing them. "Come for me. Now." Gwen smiled at his little noises of restrained pleasure as his fingers gripped her hips. He had no idea how cute his face was as he orgasmed. "Good boy." She ran her nails over his chest. "Better?"

"Mhm, but I'll feel even better in that harness you mentioned."

"Such an eager Knight." She didn't want to pull away from him yet, but they both needed to get ready. *There'll be time enough on our honeymoon.* "Time to get you dressed then." They straightened themselves out, and Gwen set about weaving the rope around Sebastian into a simple harness pattern. "Any tightness or pinching?"

"Not at all, Goddess." He snagged her hand as she moved around him one last time. "I'm so happy, and I can't wait to see you walking down the aisle towards me." He put a hand on her stomach. "And soon we'll be happy in our new home, all three of us."

"I'm happy, too, Bash. I know going to another country is going to be a big change for us, but I'm looking forward to it."

"Are you sure you're ok moving to Australia? What if you don't like it?"

"You'll be there. What's not to love?" Gwen kissed his forehead.

"You're leaving your home behind for me, everything you've ever known. You're about to be my wife and the mother of our child. With all you've given me, what could I possibly give you in return?"

"It's not a competition."

"I know."

"You've given me a lot more than you realize." She made sure her robe was closed. "Now, be a good boy and put on your tux."

"May I have another kiss?"

"For confidence," she kissed him sweetly, "that I will definitely meet you at the altar."

"Thank you, Goddess."

"See you soon, my Knight." Gwen snuck back to her room and locked the door. The impromptu session brought a bit of calm to her mind. All her luggage was packed against the end of the bed, ready to go. After the ceremony was done, they would return to their rooms to change and head out. Their mountain honeymoon was just a short drive away, and Gwen made sure to pack all the necessities, from lingerie to rope and hiking boots to gags and blindfolds. *Maybe I should've made him wear the cage for the ceremony?* "Hm. Nah. The harness is plenty. But later...."

Her smirk faltered and melted into a small frown. Even though this was what she wanted, anxiety gnawed at her. Their friends from the club were there, as was Bash's family, but there would be two empty seats right up front on her side. With no family of her own to call on, she'd asked Fabian to walk her down the aisle and be her maid of honor. *If John were still alive…. Everything is backwards.* Her heart ached. Years ago, Fabian had asked her to be the maid of honor and help with his wedding. Instead, she had to help him plan a funeral.

Knock-knock. "Dove? Can I come in?"

"Yeah, hang on." Gwen dabbed at her eyes and opened the door for Fabian. "Hey."

He shut the door quickly and lowered his voice. "What's wrong?"

"Don't worry, I'm not getting cold feet. I'm just feeling…all the feels."

"Such as?" Taking her hands, he guided her to the bed and sat down. "Tell me what's going on, babe."

Deep breath. "I wish…. I wish my grandparents were here. I wish John was here."

"Aw, ok, gentle hugs so we don't mess up the look. It's ok," he said, wrapping his arms around her shoulders. "I miss them, too, and I know they'd be happy for you. I certainly am."

"You're not jealous?"

"Over your dress? Yes. Over your marriage and happiness? Never." Fabian sighed and continued. "Yes, I'm a bit sad—wistful even —but I'm immensely happy for you. If John were here, he'd walk you down the aisle and then make a scene over handing you off to Bash."

"The dad friend."

"Haha yup. That was my man. And a dad bod to go with it." Fabian pulled back. "You love Bash, and he makes you happy. When you're with him, you glow, and if I knew nothing else about you two and your relationship, that would be enough for me. As it stands, I whole-heartedly give my blessing."

"Well, Uncle Fab better come visit often."

"Obviously. Now, let's get you dressed."

"You know, he's taking my last name. Sebastian Walsh."

"That's because he's a good little puppy," he said, rolling his eyes. "Now get over here. I need to make sure this goes on right."

I can't wait to claim Bash as my husband. Gwen giggled and the last of her nerves disappeared as Fabian helped her slip into her gown.

* * *

Red and orange leaves drifted down from the maple trees. Sebastian sighed contentedly and surveyed the grounds. Blue cushions were propped on the twenty or so white chairs flanking a narrow stone path that ended at the small dais he was standing on. Behind him, the officiator organized her notes under an archway covered with wisteria. Although they weren't in bloom this time of year, the vines were laden with golden leaves just beginning to fall. *It's a perfect day for an autumn wedding. Not too warm, not too chilly, and clear skies. Is there anything I forgot?*

Nate appeared at his side, startling him. "Your shoes are on the wrong feet."

"What?" Sebastian looked down and lifted his feet before realizing his brother was just screwing with him. "Oh, you're funny."

"'Bout time you recognized my talents." He nudged Sebastian. "Stop that."

"Stop what?"

"Worrying. Fabian and I took care of everything. 'S all gonna come good."

"I know." Sebastian flexed his fingers and tapped his foot. "Are you *sure* we're not forgetting anything?"

Nate's eyes grew wide, and he covered his mouth. "Well, now you mention it...." He put one arm around Sebastian's shoulders, steered him off to the side of the arch, and leaned in close. "Listen." He sucked in a deep breath. "I don't know how to tell you this."

"It's the ring, isn't it? You forgot the ring."

"Just shut up for a minute and listen to me, you daft bastard, I—" Nate patted around his back. "What're you wearing under your tux?"

"Never you mind. What did you forget?"

He rolled his eyes. "A stick to beat you with, dipshit. When I say Fabian and I took care of everything, I mean *everything*. You've nothing to worry about."

"But—"

"No." Nate cut him off. "Just no. I will gag you until the ceremony starts if that's what it takes."

Sebastian scowled at his brother's back as he walked off again. "Fine." *First, he's gotta be a stickybeak, now he's gotta be a sticky-ass. I'll remember this when it's his turn.* The breeze picked up, scattering more leaves, and he struggled to find a sense of calm. There was nothing left to do but wait, which quickly turned into Anxiety nagging at the back of his mind, insisting he'd forgotten *something*. He had no clue what, just that it was S O M E T H I N G. *Find your peace, Bash. You can do this. Focus.* Rope pressed comfortably across his chest and stomach before hugging his thighs and climbing up his back. Warm metal hung loosely around his right wrist—his day collar. The words inscribed on it were a source of confidence, and Sebastian soaked in the love and trust until his thoughts slowed.

"Everything right, sweetheart?"

"Yeah, mum. All good."

Debbie patted his cheek and smiled up at him proudly. "You look so handsome."

"Thanks. That's a great hat."

"Isn't it?" She adjusted her wide-brimmed, navy hat. "I thought the aqua ribbon would be a nice touch to go with the wedding colors. Is my dress too much though?" Debbie spun around quickly so the shiny navy fabric flared out slightly at her calves.

"It's perfect."

"The ceremony should be starting soon, right?"

"Mhm."

"Are you nervous?"

"A little, but it's under control. I just keep worrying I forgot something or Nate and Fab might've missed something."

"Well, don't tell your brother, but...." She glanced around and lowered her voice. "I swiped his mints. Here."

"Mum. Seriously?" Sebastian took the metal tin and stuffed it in his pocket, chuckling. "You're terrible."

"But I made you smile. Now, I'm going to sit," she said, straightening his tie. "And you just stand here looking handsome."

Debbie walked off, leaving Sebastian to his thoughts again. The seats were almost filled, and he spotted a few familiar faces from the Collared Heart—Renee, Elira, even the triplets. Melvin waved from the back row, grinning broadly with "I told you so" written all over his features. "I couldn't *not* invite him," Sebastian muttered under his breath as he returned the wave with a strained smile. They'd bumped into each other a few times at the club after the first visit, and Melvin had cackled gleefully when he found out about Sebastian and Gwen.

Suppose I should thank him at some point for dragging me out that night.

The violinist played a few bars, and everyone darted into place. Sebastian's fists clenched, and he tapped the wooden boards under his feet. *It's here. It's time. Oh shit. Ok. I'm good. Just breathe through it, Bash.* He swallowed hard and rubbed his palms together. *Everything's fine.* Someone clapped him on the shoulder. "SHIT."

"You kiss your bride with that mouth?" Nate raised his eyebrows and quickly examined Sebastian before pulling his brother's hands apart and forcing them to his sides. "Take it down a few notches, Bash. You're ok."

He was panting now. "I-I know. I...I just...I'm so...I—"

"Deep breath in, deep breath out. C'mon. You've got this." Nate maneuvered them so his brother couldn't see the guests. "In. Out. In. Out." He put one palm over Sebastian's chest and breathed with him. "There is no one else here right now. You're safe."

"But *everyone* is here," whispered Sebastian.

"Look at me and forget them. It's just us. Ok?"

"O...ok."

"Why are you here?"

"To get married."

"To whom?"

"Gwen."

"And she is?"

Sebastian shook himself and squared his shoulders. "The love of my life."

"And?"

"All that I need to be happy. Well, her and our baby."

"Ri—*what?*"

"Uh." He shrugged. "Surprise?"

Nate blinked several times. "You...utter jackass. Does mum know?"

"Nah. We were waiting to tell everyone until Gwen was a little further along."

"I'm going to be an uncle." He sucked in a breath. "You're going to be a father, and I'm going to be an uncle. Well, fuck me crossways. Congrats!"

"Thanks. Still need to get through the wedding though." Sebastian's hands shook. "Don't know how to shut this off."

"What are you afraid of? You have a gorgeous woman who loves you, an ankle biter on the way, and, if that's not enough, you're stuck with me and Mum, because we're sure as shit spoiling the hell out of that kid every chance we get."

"What if I fuck it up?"

"You've had over a year to fuck it up, and it hasn't happened yet."

"But—"

"Do you think Gwen's going to bail on you for…what?"

"No. I don't know. She accepts me, I know she does, but…."

"You can't be afraid to live your life because of a vague 'what if' that may never happen. Seize the joy that's in front of you with both hands and don't let go. You deserve it."

Sebastian paused. "Do I?"

"Bash, remember what we talked about? What did I tell you to do?" Nate scowled as his brother mumbled. "Can't hear you."

"Tell that demeaning little bastard in the back of my head to fuck off and hold onto all the reasons I have to be happy."

"Right. Well, go on. Do it. *Out loud.*"

He sucked in a deep, steadying breath and closed his eyes, focusing on the nasty voice filling him with anxiety and self-doubt. "Fuck off, you demeaning little bastard. I have a ton of reasons to be happy, and I am worthy of all I desire."

"Good. Now, you just…stand…right here," Nate said repositioning them both. "And keep telling yourself that."

"Can I open my eyes?"

"You can open your damn eyeballs when the music starts."

Sebastian muttered an insult but kept his eyes shut tight. It was easier to do if he pretended Gwen had blindfolded him. *I can open my eyes when she's walking toward me, and all I have to do is focus on her. But am I rea—no. No. I am worthy of her. I'm worthy of being happy and treated right. I'm just nervous. It's just my damn nerves. Deep, calming breaths. Find my space.* The rope harness snugged slightly when he wiggled his shoulders, pulling him back to his center.

A hush fell over the guests as the violinist began to play.

Sebastian's skin prickled. "Can I look now?" His voice was barely a whisper.

"Yes."

The music disappeared into the background, and the guests were barely a hazy mirage on the edges of his vision. Sebastian could only see one thing, one perfect image. His breath caught in his throat. *Wow.*

Gwen floated down the stone path arm in arm with Fabian, her white, strapless mermaid gown following the natural curve of her body before fading into peacock blue and swirling around her feet. Dark hair hung in loose ringlets framing her face, and several blue somethings sparkled around her neck. She'd chosen not to wear a veil, so Sebastian saw clearly she wasn't looking anywhere but at him. Gwen's gaze was steady, her stride confident, and her lips as blue and as quick to smirk as the first time he saw her.

"Hello, handsome," she said softly when she stood in front of him.

"H-hi." Sebastian felt his cheeks burning and barely heard the part where Fabian announced he was giving her away. He held her hands gently and thought his heart would burst.

"Ahem. We are gathered here today," the officiator began, moving effortlessly through the first part of the ceremony. No one objected, although Fabian sniffled loudly over Gwen's shoulder and dabbed at his eyes. "I believe the couple has chosen to write their own vows. Gwen?"

She took a black band from Fabian. "I wasn't sure where things might go when we met. I was afraid when I wanted more, when I felt more, that you might not want or feel those things, too. Nevertheless, you stayed beside me and didn't balk at my scars. I'm humbled by your love and devotion, and so I happily take you as my husband to bind, gag, and sweetly torture for the rest of my days. I vow to guide, protect, and dominate you in all capacities to which you willingly and knowingly consent, with the utmost respect for your safety, sovereignty, and trust. I vow to lift you up and support you, to be the one you can always rely on, and to do everything in my power to be worthy of your trust and love." The ring slipped snuggly on his finger.

"Sebastian?"

"Yes." He vibrated with excitement and nerves as he took the white-gold band Nate handed him. "When I first met you, I was lost. You walked up to me so confident and radiant, and I *knew* something was happening, but I couldn't begin to suspect how deeply and profoundly you would affect my life. I am eternally grateful for everything and everyone that brought us together. Thank you for taking a chance on me—on us. I eagerly take you as my wife, the woman I desire to worship, cherish, and kneel before for the rest of my days. I vow to never demand more than you are willing to give, to never touch you in anger, and to always respect your boundaries. I vow to listen to your joys and sorrows, to support you in all things, to be honest and upfront, and to give you all that I am as both submissive and partner." Fingers trembling slightly, Sebastian slid the ring on.

"Then by the power vested in me, I pronounce you wife and husband. You may kiss."

Gwen and Sebastian embraced while their guests applauded. They had made it, and while they couldn't know what the future held for them, they trusted they would face it together.

And they lived kink-ily ever after.

<u>Some Australian Colloquialisms and Their Meanings</u>

Wowser – Someone who sucks the fun out of a situation, also used for a person who wants to deprive others of the joys of any behavior deemed sinful or immoral.

Ocker – He's uncultured and boorish, babes.

True blue – Genuine, loyal. This also seems to be used to indicate authenticity, especially if something is being espoused as authentically Australian.

Fair dinkum – Stating something as being fair or true.

Pash – Kiss.

I couldn't really find a consistently reliable guide to Aussie terms online. I even consulted with a couple of people who are Australian and didn't necessarily get consistency. A lot of terms depend on where someone is from in Australia, and many others are more generational. It was certainly educational.

<u>Some Welsh Pronunciations</u>

Dd – So, the double-d gives us a "th" sound, like in the, there, and they.

W – If it's between consonants, it's a vowel. The short vowel sound is an "uh" while the long vowel is "oo". If it's with a vowel then it's a consonant that sounds like "w."

Ll – You know what, I don't really know what to tell you with this one. I'm sure I say it wrong, but it kind of comes off as almost making the "l" sound but with a "heh" at the same time.

Ch – Think of "Loch Ness." Does not sound like charity or chirp.

F – This sounds like a "v," which is why Afon (the word for river) is pronounced Avon.

Ff – Actually makes the usual "f" sound that we're familiar with in English.

U – This one is…yeah, it's pronounced like an "I."

I – This sounds like an "I" unless it's in front of another vowel, in which case it makes more of a "y" sound as in "yesterday."

R – Always pronounce the "r" and always roll it.

For something more complete, I recommend going online and finding a straightforward guide attached to a reliable Welsh-English dictionary.

www.ingramcontent.com/pod-product-compliance
Lightning Source LLC
Chambersburg PA
CBHW071320130726

47996CB00002B/557